HARVEST

The Rhys Davies
Short Story Award Anthology

Jane Fraser lives in Llangennith on the Gower peninsula, south Wales. She is the author of two collections of short fiction, *The South Westerlies* (2019) and *Connective Tissue* (2022), published by SALT. Her debut novel, *Advent* (2021), published by HONNO, was awarded the Society of Authors' Paul Torday Memorial Prize in 2022.

Her short stories have been placed highly in major international competitions including the Manchester Fiction Prize (finalist 2017), the ABR Elizabeth Jolley Prize, and the Fish and Rhys Davies Short Story Prizes.

Her work has appeared in *New Welsh Review*, *The Lonely Crowd* and *The London Magazine* as well as being broadcast on BBC Radio 4.

She has an MA and PhD in Creative Writing from Swansea University and is a Hay Festival Writer at Work.

Jane has recently been awarded a Society of Authors' grant to work on her latest novel: an intergenerational, ecofeminist story set in Gower.

Twitter @jfraserwriter | Instagram @janefraserwriter | www.jane fraserwriter.com

Originally from Belfast, Elaine Canning is a public engagement specialist, writer and editor living in Swansea, south Wales. She holds an MA and PhD in Hispanic Studies from Queen's University, Belfast and an MA in Creative Writing from Swansea University. She is currently Head of Special Projects at Swansea University, including the international Dylan Thomas Prize. As well as having written a monograph and papers on Spanish Golden-Age drama, she has published several short stories. Her debut novel, *The Sandstone City*, was published by Aderyn Press in 2022. She is also editor of *Maggie O'Farrell: Contemporary Critical Perspectives* (forthcoming, Bloomsbury, 2023). She is a member of the British Council Wales' Advisory Committee and a Fellow of the Learned Society of Wales. Twitter: @elaine_canning.

HARVEST

The Rhys Davies
Short Story Award Anthology

Edited by Elaine Canning
Selected and Introduced
by Jane Fraser

Parthian, Cardigan SA43 1ED
www.parthianbooks.com
ISBN 978-1-914595-74-5
First published in 2023 © the contributors
Edited by Elaine Canning
Cover design by Syncopated Pandemonium
Typeset by Elaine Sharples www.typesetter.org.uk
Printed by 4edge Limited
Printed on FSC accredited paper

Contents

Introduction

Jane Fraser

I hold my hand up that I came to the work of Rhys Davies later in life than I would have wished. However, it was not too late thanks to award-winning Welsh author, friend and former short story mentor, Jon Gower. It was Jon who signposted me to the Rhys Davies Short Story Conference held at Swansea University in 2013: an event dedicated to one of Wales's most prolific prose writers. Here I discovered that during his career, Blaenclydach-born Rhys Davies (1901 – 1978) wrote more than one hundred short stories, in addition to twenty novels, three novellas, two topographical books about Wales, two plays and an autobiography.

Looking back, this was a pivotal few days at the early stages of my personal writing journey, a few days where I made further discoveries about the creative possibilities of the short story genre, and reinforced my belief that the short story was a beautifully compressed and controlled art form, its writing no way an apprenticeship to writing a novel.

Following the conference, I immersed myself in Davies's short stories, drawn in by the feelings of loss, loneliness, longing and the search for identity, inclusion and belonging, exhibited in his characters, especially women. He wrote of life's 'outsiders' in Wales from his perspective as a gay man, living in exile in London at a time when homosexuality was a criminalised offence. With the lost and the lonely came humour and a keen ear for comedic dialogue. It was a powerful combination: what I came to term 'the Rhys Davies effect'.

To be asked to guest-judge the 2023 Rhys Davies National Short Story Competition (the tenth in its history) is therefore a privilege and a pleasure. It is both subjective and objective: subjective in that I can empathise with the entrants' desires to correspond with a reader on the page, perhaps for the first time in their writing careers, and objective at the same time, having to identify those anonymous writers who demonstrate excellence in the territory of the short story: theme; characterisation; point of view; tone of voice; control of the narrative; effective handling of time – where to begin and where to end; the power of the unsaid; and the 'feeling' that the short story leaves behind after the last sentence is read. And that indefinable, magical relationship between writer and reader. I wanted to read stories where I could feel the writer taking an in-breath at the beginning, sense the energy being maintained throughout, and where the out-breath at the end gave me a feeling of satisfaction, even though that ending might not be tied up. All this in a maximum of five thousand words.

What I was looking for can perhaps be better expressed by the wonderful short story writer, George Saunders, who says that short stories are 'the deep, encoded crystallisations of all human knowledge. They are rarefied dense meaning machines shedding light on the most pressing of life's dilemmas.' I wanted stories that would enable me to understand what it *feels* like to be human. No artifice. No sentimentality. Rather, authentic and emotional truth. And it was this truth I found prevalent among the thematic concerns in the twelve stories I selected.

The themes of loss and longing figure highly in many of the stories. 'Nos Da, Popstar' by Joshua Jones, sees a girl dreaming of winning a talent show, but the restrained subtext makes it clear and without drama, that this is not what she is really wanting. The story creates an authentic sense of contemporary pop culture and a real sense of a working-class area of Llanelli – heightened by the writer's keen eye for signposts in the landscape and a keen ear for authentic dialogue and the vernacular. So too, in Rachel Powell's 'Bricks and Sticks' we see the female protagonist longing for what has passed, and anticipating grief that is yet to come in a house that holds love and family memories. The writer takes the domestic and the apparently ordinary and conjures a tale that is universal, full of feeling and most definitely, extraordinary.

Regret, resentment and the life not lived are the themes of Dan Williams's powerful story, 'The Nick of Time', set in Trwm Ddu (Heavy Black) Powys, where the external landscape and the internal thoughts of one of the central characters seem intertwined. The narrative simmers with rising tension and claustrophobia as it comes to the boil. Set in Wales (or 'your land' as one of the story's characters refers to it) 'Welcome to Momentum 2023' by Emily Vanderploeg is an ironic exploration of 'outsider' perspectives on Wales. Tone of voice is maintained throughout this wry story of the loss of cultural traditions and language and Wales selling its soul as a theme park. 'Save the Maiden' by Bethan L. Charles revisits a tale from Welsh folklore in a timeless story of apocalyptic floods, maidens and monsters, told with a feminist twist. The rhythm of the prose is wonderful, and the language beautifully wrought.

'We Shall All Be Changed' by Satterday Shaw and 'The Pier' by Emma Moyle both have interesting perspectives. The young, science-loving female protagonist in the former 'doesn't know how she feels' and employs her peculiar logic when she encounters the dead body of a woman in Coed Felin. The close third person narration employs a register that translates the character aptly. In the latter, an omniscient, multi-perspective journalistic/reportage story, darkness and menace play out in a one-day time frame on the pier and amusement arcade in Wales, with security cameras used effectively as characters offering an additional point of view to the events that take place. The pace and tone are arresting and immediate, down to the use of the present tense.

'Fish Market' by Silvia Rose and Ruby Burgin's 'Kind Red Spirit' take the reader out of Wales through stories set respectively in Spain and Japan. In 'Fish Market' we have a skilled narrator creating an atmospheric sense of place in a sensual and deeply moving tale of impending loss during a couple's mini-break in a Spanish city. Burgin's 'Kind Red Spirit' is a contemplative story of grief and ultimate acceptance. I loved the symbolism, dripping with colour, and the way the writer moves effortlessly from realism to magic realism within a controlled narrative arc.

'Second to Last Rites' by Ruairi Bolton employs classic oral storytelling techniques alongside contemporary stylistic features. The story explores the liminal space between life and death, as well as the relationship between grief and memory, with a good dollop of rare and much-needed humour.

'Sunny Side Up' crafted by JL George, takes Rhys Davies's birthplace of the Rhondda and fast-forwards it to the day of Queen Elizabeth II's funeral in 2022. Set over breakfast in a café, this is a visceral and political dissection of post-industrial south Wales seen through the eyes of a disaffected and disillusioned young man, Billy Ferretti, an 'outsider' in his own community. This is mature, polished and informed writing.

I selected 'Harvest' by Matthew G. Rees as my winning

4

story. It takes the reader deep into the territory of the short story as exemplified by Rhys Davies. Here we see a man exiled by his belligerence, attempting to hold back time's march. The liminal space of the cockle-beds is not a mere backdrop, but a living, breathing habitat for Cock Davies to enact his final almost Biblical denouement and act of self-destruction. The narrative structure is controlled, the language archaic and delicious, the voice distinctive.

Thanks to the Rhys Davies Trust and the Rhys Davies National Short Story Competition, these dozen stories will be able to – and deserve to – be read by the many. Their authors represent the wide range of confident, accomplished and diverse modern-day voices that have presented themselves in 2023. I'd like to think Rhys Davies would be pleased with his legacy.

Harvest

Matthew G. Rees

Gull wing-grey sky, tide sucked lower than his good eye can see, Cock Davies rides his tractor down the slip. Hair wild as windswept saltmarsh, face an arrowhead of fierce-cut flint, his calloused hands clench the wheel of his old, phutting Fordson like crab claws. Silurian charioteer of the sort who fought the Romans. All that's lacking is the warpaint, as he lands on the sands of the estuary.

And his mood – jounce and rattle of his tow-hooked trailer behind him, black soot clouds storming from his tractor's steepling pipe – *is* war-like.

Steamrollering the shells of the strandline, he surveys the estuary for signs of life, especially other pickers. Memory of that morning's collision with 'officialdom' swelling – red-raw – within him, like an unrazorbladed boil.

'Back again, Mr Davies?' the girl on the council's counter had said.

In her sing-song voice, a ring of wonder-come-mockery – to the ears of Davies, at least – that he, Old Cock, had survived another winter and should be there at all.

'All this ought really to be done online now, you know,' she'd continued, as he'd pushed his terse note – '*Hoffwn adnewyddu fy nhrwydded* ('I wish to renew my licence'), D. Davies' – under her screen.

Visible on the sheet's upper: the inscription in English as

7

decreed by his great-great-grandfather, Solomon Emlyn, lauded cockler of the Davies line, possessor of the beard of an Old Testament prophet, and the most expert 'in-the-field' (rather than mere *academic*) authority, to those who knew shellfish, in the whole of the land of Wales.

Finest Welsh Cockles. Since 1750.

The words said only what was needed, as was the Davies way – and in a font and tar-darkness that offered no compromise.

Along with the note: Davies's payment – a sum the signing away of which had caused him to wince.

'Paying by cheque, is it?' the girl had asked, as if – to *his* ears – this was some huge inconvenience… as if he'd proposed settlement in shillings and crowns, or with a sewin still dripping, rabbits (limp of neck) and widgeon, warm, bill-bloodied and lead-flecked.

The girl had continued: 'Card facilities *are* available on our app, Mr —'

At which point, he'd intervened. 'That's the right money,' he'd said of his cheque. 'To the penny. Don't you worry about that.'

On the screen – bilingually – between them was a notice that annoyed him: 'WE WILL <u>NOT</u> TOLERATE ABUSE OF OUR STAFF'.

This was new, Davies thought. He had no recollection of it from previous years.

And it seemed to Davies as if it had been put there *for him*… as if they – the bloody bureaucrats – had known *he'd* be coming… renewing – cockling's equivalent of the stitchwort of the coastal swards… the sharks that newspapers said basked off the bay come summer… the rheumatism that returned to his knees with the autumn rains… the chilblains that troubled his fingertips and toes in winter frosts.

Feeling the obligation, his onslaught had then begun. '*Not* that the thing is worth having. Licence?! Be damned!! This council has made a *desert* of that estuary! You can't move on those sands for pickers. Every Jack and Jill… forking and raking. Like ants, they are… crawling all over. *Destroyed*, those beds have been. *Over*-harvested! All thanks to *this* place. The cockles have never had a chance!'

Davies had wanted to say how – up in England – there was a term for what was left of the beds now, after the pillage and the plunder: *Cock All* (not that he had ever *been* to England… this phrase being merely a scrap of the kind that, when encountered, he was prone to seize on – like some angry cat or scavenger gull).

He'd held back on his language though, sensing he'd said enough. Enough to get a letter of the kind he'd had before, written by some soft-handed, collar-and-tie, warm radiator-in-my-office, cup-of-coffee-on-my-desk, parasitical *managerial* type. Taking home sixty thousand – to be sure. Who knew nothing about cockles, of course.

'You have my address,' Davies had – instead – said (for the delivery of his permit… and – if need be – the idiot letter from the 'executive' too timid to speak man-to-man). 'We've been there two hundred and seventy years, if not longer.'

And then he'd walked out to where he'd left his tractor – in some damn fool official's space – in the car park.

There may be rain, Davies thinks, riding over the sand. The sky has 'the look'. Although a drop has yet to fall, he can smell it in the air… taste it on his tongue. Here and there, seabirds catch his eye: an egret on the edge of a channel; a low-flying cormorant, feathers mere feet from the flats. Occasionally, there is a judder from the trailer behind him, on which his tools rest and sometimes bounce – his shovel, his rake, his sieve, his sacks. That disturbance (and the engine of the Fordson) apart, he relishes the silence – and stillness – of the sands. Their empty infinity calms him. Here he is both alone *and* at home... with his kin. On such days, he not infrequently sees their ghosts: women in aprons and shawls, whiskered men with horses – or donkeys – and carts; all toiling quietly, save perhaps some words in Welsh, an equine snort or whinny. And then gone: taken by sea fret... some shimmer of sun.

Suddenly, from his Fordson's worn-smooth seat, Davies sees figures... *rival* pickers... assembled on a bank. And not *any* bank, but one of 'his'. They also have seen *him*... and cease raking.

They eye him.

In Davies's eyes: bandits; mercenaries; the ragtag irregulars of some marauding army.

He wonders why, on this particular expedition, he hasn't noticed them till now... and worries for a moment about the sharpness of his senses.

He attributes the failure of his antennae to the nonsense with the council, the pain of the cheque – the tithe unfairly (as he sees it) exacted so that he might be here, on *his* ground.

Before now, he and they – the other pickers – have had words. 'These are *my* beds,' he has told them, with anger and spittle (in English as well as Welsh).

But they have stood their ground.

Outnumbered, he has retreated.

And now, resting on their rakes and forks, they watch him... as if wondering what he will say, or do, next.

This stand-off is conducted at a distance: Davies having halted the Fordson, so that it idles, roughly, beneath him.

He sits there: high, lean, *territorial*, like some ancient, starved heron of the shore.

A breeze tugs at the loose flaps of his oilskins.

Although angered by their 'piracy' (as he feels it to be), he is aware that they are many and that he is one (even allowing for the reputation that he knows rides with him). Besides, he has heard – before now – of clubs, knives and even guns being drawn.

He lets out the clutch of the Fordson, gives them wide berth, rides on (consoling himself that he will find better beds, bigger cockles, and that to do so is his birthright; it is in his bones, his blood).

In truth, though, he has doubts. In his mind, the words Ionwen Pryce used of his last batch (in a phone call from her stall at the market): 'On the small side this week, Mr Davies.'

After her, he hears the voice of his great-great-grandfather, Solomon Emlyn – who Davies never knew, but who speaks to him in dreams. 'Ein *cocos ni yw'r gorau, fachgen. Cofia hynny.*' ('*Our* cockles are the best, boy. Remember that.') These words uttered now not in a tone of reminding but of chiding, as if Davies has been failing his forebears, as if 'S.E.' – beneath his mossed and lichened chest tomb – has got wind of the grumbles of Ionwen Pryce.

All of which now causes Davies, albeit somewhat apprehensive over his reserves of diesel (and a possible change in the weather), to drive deeper into the estuary's gaping emptiness than he has ever foraged before.

Rags of blue and white reveal themselves, like ill-strung laundry, in the otherwise slate-coloured sky. Conscious of his remoteness, Davies is encouraged by the seeming brightening of conditions, wary as he knows he must be of the peculiarity of the estuary and its world. 'Out there' lay no shelter. The sands were like Mars, his father had once warned him: a capricious climate all of the estuary's own. One cockler – long-buried in a coastal yard – had been struck dead by lightning. Burnt to a cinder, so help him, where the poor fellow had stood – a human rod to that furious fork… *there*… on the sand. All that remained: his rake's charred iron – this, rather than any human flesh and bones, being buried in his coffin in the wind-scarred cemetery of that bitter-cold church on its cliff.

His spirits buoyed by the sunlight spilling over the shoulders of clouds, Davies, in the saddle of the Fordson, veers yet further from the slender and disappearing shore. He crosses flatlands, ascends and descends sandbanks, fords channels of fresh and saltwater – his air redolent of a lone prospector, driving a waggon on some old-time – and less trodden – Western trail.

On a wet and non-descript flat that is more mud than sand, Davies suddenly stops… miles, even leagues, from the shore.

There are no outward, above-ground, signs – no 'casts' as with lugworms, no 'keyholes' as with razor clams, nor even any shells that have been split open and abandoned by birds.

But, in his bones, Davies *knows*.

For several moments, he simply holds still.

Then he arcs the Fordson around.

As he does so, he looks back at the coast… or where he thinks the coast must lie. Its seam is now so narrow as to barely be the line of a baited hook; its houses and buildings – the church, the chapel, Idwal Evans's garage, The Admiral's Arms (in its paint of bird's egg blue) – mere pinheads, if that.

Davies feels sure no one has ever been this far out, but he looks left and right, even so… eyes alive to anything that might move.

His thumb and forefinger (needing no guidance: they know their way) turn the ignition key to 'Off'.

Faintly, very faintly, Davies's ears – his lobes ugly, leathery, weather-bitten things – hear the falling of waves… a sound that, given the uncommonly deep retreat of the sea on this section of coast, tells him he is distant from dry land indeed.

The remoteness of the shore means that it is difficult for him to make a precise fix on his location. But he knows that he has left the estuary's throat… maybe also its mouth… with the possibility that where he now lies is – save for him – the unfilled bed of the sea.

He twists in his seat and peers for water… discerning, with the aid of a break in the cloud cover, a distant and copper-like *llyn*, which – as the sky above it alters – flashes then vanishes, as quickly as it has appeared…

Davies dismounts the Fordson.

Saltwater spits from beneath his old boots.

Fleetingly, a rainbow (or part of one) shows.

Not someone normally given to romantic thought (a man more of clouds than silver linings), Davies takes its rings for a portent: the possibility that – alone as a rock stack whose monument has been shunned by seabirds – he may be standing on buried treasure.

Davies begins with two boards that he takes from the bed of his trailer. The centimetre or so of seawater above the sand suggests he may not need them (since any cockles – if shellfish there should be – will be sited near the moist surface). But he decides that, having brought the boards, he will deploy them. He lays them down flat, then walks on the wood... in something approaching a dance (his disturbance – hopefully – 'waking' what he thinks awaits him... down below).

More so than on other days, there is something self-hypnotising in his shuffles and his strides.

At first, all is normal enough. But, to his escalating unease, his 'jig' seems to conjure voices. The tones are those of women... women he knows from old pictures: cockle-sellers.

His turns and his stamps elicit strange, siren calls. *Who will buy our cockles? Who will buy? Who will buy?*

And Davies – seldom less than certain, imperious even, on these sands, *his* lands – is unnerved. A single – and singular – man, he has always been wary of women – mindful, in a tight-lipped way, of tales of sailors who've fallen among mermaids... to wake in the clutches of hags.

He spins round, as if to surprise would-be assailants – perhaps the pirate pickers, who might have followed him at a distance, concealing themselves in channels, lying low behind sandbanks.

Spinning and stopping... and spinning again, he is like some distempered dog in pursuit of its tail.

For all his agitation, he sees nothing... except a few tongues of mist and the empty, and seemingly unending, flats.

Davies does what he can to compose himself, wondering whether he might not be 'losing it' (in the way he has heard of lonely men: keepers of lighthouses, shepherds of mountain flocks).

He raises his hands and ruffles such scant slack that exists in the flesh of his face (his skin is dry and trimmed tight, like a wind-scoured strip of old sail).

Lowering his palms, he looks up at the sky.

Never one to have worn a wristwatch (the tides, moon and sun have always been his clocks), his eyes search for the latter's orb… or some sign of it.

With effort, he locates in the grey and whale-heavy heavens a ragged rockpool of light.

Its position tells him the sun is dipping… that the hour is well past noon. This knowledge causes him to wonder how far he has come, the wisdom of what he has done (and is doing).

'Rhaid i mi frysio nawr,' ('I must hurry now,') he tells himself. *'Mae'r tywod yn llithro trwy'r gwydr.'* ('The sand is slipping through the glass.')

In appearance, his rake is an ugly, hideous thing: a sort-of outsized cockerel claw of three pig-iron prongs that curve cruelly inwards, its neck the socket for a staff of some uncertain wood that rises crooked as the climb of a mountain goat, and whose colour has become coal-like. Never mind how the years have polished eel-smooth its knobbles and its knots, it seems to have 'eyes' that lurk on – and look from – its long, black rod. A tool to uncover cockles, to be sure… and one that, if need be, could (comfortably) maim – and even kill – a man.

This 'instrument' is the source of the nickname by which Davies is known (to those other pickers whose families are sufficiently ancient and engrained in the estuary for him to half acknowledge).

Ceiliog.

In English, a coincidental truncation of that which he seeks: Cock.

Not that there are many who have actually seen the relic. Wise as it may be deemed *not* to work the sands alone, Davies always has… there seeming something of the farmyard fowl about his shape, his manner, in the eyes of those who've glimpsed him: dark, distant, a belligerence barely suppressed, an inborn need to rule the roost. You wouldn't pick a fight with an old bird like Davies. Never mind his moulted feathers and his mounting years, his spurs were still *scythe*-sharp.

To him, his trident is sacred. There is no older rake on the estuary. It has been willed down through history, from one Davies to the next. When he holds it, he has the conviction that not even Old Neptune is his equal. For *he* is Cock Davies… sea lord… suzerain… king.

He removes it from the trailer with reverence… as if it were the wand of Myrddin, the sword of Arthur, the golden cane of Henry Tudor, the furled umbrella of David Lloyd George. Having done so, he steps solemnly to the scene of his cockle-dance… on the crust of the sand and the mud.

A prayer of a kind – '*Am yr hyn yr wyf ar fin ei dderbyn…*' ('For what I am about to receive…') – passes over his lips, thin as the marram that spikes dune summits… dry as old bladderwrack heaped high on the shore.

And now, from above his head – beneath a Turner seascape sky, a shade darker than those of the artist's eighteenth-century tours – he swings down his claw… into the sediment.

The entire estuary seems to shudder.

With a drag of the rake, Davies uncovers the first cockle… albeit its nature does not initially suggest 'shellfish'.

Its freakish size causes Davies to presume it a pebble, or even, bizarrely, a potato.

Only on lifting it and wiping away the surrounding sand and muck does he see, and register, the shells.

He looks again at what he holds, rubs it anew… sees the ribs… feels the beak… stares at it, in wonder.

The find *occupies* his palm… like a soap bar.

It is the largest he has ever seen.

From his oilskins, Davies – who is quite dumbfounded – manages to draw a pocketknife.

Like his rake, this is an heirloom that has been passed down, from one Davies to the next. Its handle: narwhal horn, so earlier Davieses have sworn (though his suspicions have long been of the headwear of a four-legged field-dwelling beast).

It bears a grimed scrimshaw of a ship's ringlet-haired figurehead – this being the closest Cock has ever come to holding a woman (an indifference that may be mutual); the estuary has been his wife… his life.

He pulls out a grey and far from sharp sheepsfoot blade, whose bevel and back show scars of long service. He works its end into the cockle, sawing at the fibrous ligament between the shells.

These are reluctant to separate. But, in time, and with persistence, they part.

Davies now quickly puts away the knife and continues to prise, with his fingers and thumbs.

Like the case of some seized and rusted pocket watch, the shells, finally, yield.

Davies is astonished by what he sees inside. For his eyes – rimmed red by the rub of decades of sand grains and sea salt – meet not the small morsel of flesh to which, in more than half a century of cockle-picking, as boy and man, they have grown accustomed, but something that lies spread… like a breakfast egg – a goose egg in girth, at that… and sitting as if in a pan; its 'yolk', it might be said, imbued with the most glorious golden *glow*.

It's as if Davies hasn't raked a mere cockle from the estuary's bed but has reached up and raked down the sun.

Davies considers it with awe. He wonders if his ancestors ever saw such a thing. He decides that they couldn't have, for what he has found, he tells himself, is the mollusc equivalent of the kind of diamond that bejewels a maharajah's crown... a match for the most fabulous nugget of any goldminer's fevered dreams.

He wonders what to do with it.

He again looks around him, over the sands... sees that they lie empty, as before.

There can be only *one* course of action, he decides. Besides: the cockle (prised open, as it has been) will be dead, 'unfit', by the time he has returned to dry land.

And so, he raises the shell to his lips... and he fingers its moist flesh into the cragged sea cave of his mouth.

Some are cautious about shellfish, especially the eating of them 'raw'. But, on that count, Davies has no worries. His is the gullet of the sea crow, the iron stomach of the shark.

Fear, anyway, is uncalled for.

For it is the finest cockle that Davies has ever tasted – that *any* man can ever have tasted. To his mouth and his mind: a symphony of sensations defiant of true description, but... *soft* as a barn owl's down, *meaty* as a shoulder of mutton, and possessed of the *tingle* of a mountain trout, as it plays among the tobacco-brown stumps of his teeth and swims over the shallow dams of his shrivelled gums.

It is molten gold in his maw.

The swallowing of it – '*Dduw, Melys!*' ('God, Sweet!') – brings an ecstasy. It is as if his whole being undergoes a miraculous alchemy: a gorgeous, deity-given delight that sweeps through him, to the tips of his fingers, toes, wrinkled nose, and member. He feels himself immortal... god-like, in that paradise of the sands.

But then, as if he has stood witness to the most wonderful sunset, the elation ebbs. And he is seized by a sadness: that such a moment shall never be repeated… that he will never see – or taste – a cockle of its like again…

Sensing that its shells shall become treasure (an heirloom, like his knife and rake), he stows them in a pocket of his oilskins – proof, if challenged (not that there are many on the estuary who dare to cross *Ceiliog*), of the veracity of his tale.

For several moments, he stands, as if spellbound, on the immense sedimental plain.

Then he raises his claw to the heavens… and brings it down again.

To Davies's amazement, the draw of his rake uncovers a crop of cockles equal in size – and perhaps even larger – than the first.

He falls to his knees in disbelief.

He scrabbles… lifts them to his eyes, as if surveying Spanish doubloons.

Pam? (Why?) he wonders. *Sut?* (How?)

Ar beth maen nhw'n bwydo? (On what do they feed?)

He tries to make sense of how this hoard lies *here*… in a bed uncharted by his ancestors, harvesters of cockles in the estuary since William the Conqueror's time and probably before. In a drawer of a dresser in Davies's cottage: documents with the cracked wax seals of lords and shrieves; immaculate ledgers of his forebears; accounts of cockles picked – decade after decade, century upon century… dates, weights, and prices fetched (of course).

Yet of *this* bed, not a word…

It can only be the doing of The Almighty, Davies – no attender of chapel or church – concedes.

Supporting himself with the shaft of his rake, he rises from his knees and quickly takes a bucket and sieve from the trailer.

Bending back to the sand, he scoops the cockles into the bucket – partly with the rake's claw, partly with his human one. The yield from that single sweep almost fills the pail.

Other than sloughing off sand, there's no real need for his sieve.

The size of *these* cockles means there's no risk of any proving too small, slipping through the net.

Davies empties them into a sack snatched from the trailer. Still awed by their size, he wonders what they will be worth… on the tables of fancy restaurants… served with best bacon for breakfast in 'lounges' of hotels – places where even the proprietors deign to see him when he has something 'special' (tradesmen's door, of course – never mind that *his* tribe predates all of them, and that he is *Ceiliog*, the estuary's king).

He sets down the sack on the trailer and returns with his rake to the sand. He claws at the sediment again… and, to his astonishment, unearths *another* king-sized crop.

These he adds – in a state of both incredulity and joy – to those he has already bagged.

Davies now digs afresh with his rake, and the same thing happens – again and again… until all of his sacks on his trailer are full.

Never has he known such a bounteous harvest… such a beautiful day.

Kneeling on the sand, Davies continues to stuff as many cockles as will fit in the pockets of his oilskins, which now balloon and sag about him, like saddlebags on a mule.

He struggles to stand, under his coat's straining weight, but does so… just.

Walking awkwardly, he comes level with his tractor and,

using all of his wiry, wily strength, he levers himself into the seat of the Fordson.

As he sits, there is a scrape-come-clatter of the shells that he bears... as if in strange – and ugly – imitation of a Morris dancer's bells.

His attention moves, though, to something more pressing. For, as Davies readies for the off, he feels the Fordson sink... its chassis go down in the sand.

And, for the first time, in all of that afternoon, he becomes aware of the great burden with which he has saddled his old workhorse.

Another matter then arrests his attention. From behind him, albeit at some distance, he hears waves – rhythmic, falling; the 'roar' of water.

It is the sound of the estuary's tide... coming in.

With an unpleasant shift in the bilgewater of his bladder, Davies now remembers something that, in the excitement of his harvest, he has, till that moment, forgotten: his unusually long distance from the shore.

Davies turns the key of the Fordson. The tractor fires first time. He leans forward and pats a rusty panel of engine housing. *'Merch dda,'* ('Good girl,') he says and then adds, as if to reassure: *'Byddwn adref cyn bo hir, ti a fi.'* ('We'll be home soon, you and me.')

Smoke plumes from the pipe in front of him, sand spits from the rubber tyres of the rear wheels.

The tractor, though – never mind Davies's engagement of gears and throttle – doesn't budge (beyond a sort-of early – and abandoned – half lunge).

Weighed down by his coat of cockles, the shells scrunching at his sides, Davies cannot see to what exact extent the tractor and trailer have become embedded.

21

He knows that a lack of traction is the problem. He also knows the ancient nature of his machine, which was his grandfather's (and likely someone else's before) – and that, above all, he must *not* burn anything out.

He turns off the ignition; the Fordson shudders... and is silent.

Davies now begins counting and, as he does so, he looks up at the sky. It has grown darker, and he again remembers the rain he smelt on setting out. Meanwhile, behind him, he hears the sea. It is louder, closer now, than was the case, and, to his ears, its tone is faintly... mocking.

'*Naw ar ddeugain...*' ('Nine on two twenties...') Davies counts aloud. '*Hanner cant.*' ('Fifty.')

He refires the Fordson. The tractor starts. It shifts under him somewhat, but seems only to dig itself deeper. There is no go-forward, no 'pull'.

'*Mae ei cheffylau i gyd ar y môr,*' ('Her horses are all at sea,') thinks Davies.

And he wants to curse... oh, *how* he wans to curse... to bring down – from his pulpit-perch on the Fordson – raging fire and brimstone. On the idiotic council and its ridiculous 'executives'. On the haughty hoteliers and their gluttonous guests. On the pirate pickers who pillaged and plundered his birthright. On Ionwen Pryce, all uppity at her stall in the market, for her slight about his cockles '*bychan*' ('small').

And yet...

He bites that scathing, flaying, Old Testament tongue, and instead entreats his tractor with the softest, sweetest words he can summon.

'*Dewch ymlaen, gariad,*' ('Come on, darling,') he whispers. '*Dewch ymlaen, ferch,*' ('Come on, girl,') he says.

The tractor seems to hear him – and answers.

Man and machine begin to rock... forwards and backwards... out of and into that curve of moist sand... until – like a Cob foal from a bed of straw – she rises and lifts the two of them... free.

Cock Davies and his cargo are moving... homeward bound.

He is king of the estuary, re-crowned.

Some yards and minutes on, Davies, in dimming light, enters a district of the flats where the sand and mud is like a mire. It's as if the seawater which he knows to be at his back has slyly risen through the land ahead of him.

The Fordson halts: wheels and axles bogged.

Davies senses in the tractor a nervousness – an almost animalistic intuiton – of something that seems to lie in wait.

The tractor's stutters and groans tell him what, in his heart, he knows: that he must lighten the load.

With some difficulty, given the cockle-burdened weight of his coat, he climbs from the Fordson's seat and onto the trailer. From there, he lifts and slings one sack of cockles to the left and another to the right. He stands on the trailer and watches for a moment as the sacks begin to sink... hearing the *suck* of the wet sand and mud, as the estuary claims her cockles back.

The sacrifice proves sufficient to free up the Fordson.

Davies drives on.

Within fifty yards, he's labouring again. The sand – although it should be solid now – is glutinous. And he begins to wonder... He *is* shore-bound, isn't he? Those lights, that he seems to see, *are* on land and *aren't* of boats in the bay?

This time he throws over two sacks to the left and two to the right. The rain that he'd feared begins: beating his face... and the increasingly bare bed of the trailer.

He journeys on but is forced into an ongoing abandonment of his cargo, jettisoning his sacks, as if over the sides of a boat… from the basket of a balloon… till the very last one of them is gone.

'*Fy nghynhaeaf! Fy nghynhaeaf hardd!*' ('My harvest! My beautiful harvest!') his scarecrow shape cries out, in soaked and battered oilskins, on his trailer's empty bed.

Yet he consoles himself: that he will get home, that he will survive, that he knows where to rake… next time.

He tells himself he is *still* the estuary's lord and master… *Ceiliog*… its king.

In the darkening twilight, on an area of the flats that Davies finds unfamiliar, the Fordson drinks its last diesel, staggers and then stops.

Soon, seawater is surging against its wheels and axles… ascending unto *Ceiliog*, where he holds court on his cold throne.

Aloft: his rake's dark sceptre.

The estuary encases him – its climbing tide, its lowering sky – as if he were in its shells.

Sunny Side Up

JL George

In London and on the TV above the counter they are burying the Queen, and in Suzy's All-American Diner, deep in the arsecrack of the Rhondda, Billy Ferretti is ordering breakfast.

Out of habit, he studies the chalkboard menu that hasn't changed in six years. The glass that separates the kitchen from the rest of the diner reflects back a street shuttered and silent as a Sunday in the eighties, empty but for a couple of teenagers walking a grey-muzzled staffie and Denny Lewis the pisshead waiting across the street for a bus that won't come. Sleepy unease blankets the valley and everyone outside in it — outside in defiance of the great and pious communion taking place across the land right now, settees turned mourning benches, TV signals interlocking like prayerful hands. You could be forgiven for thinking it was magic, mass hypnosis, an occult ritual.

You could be forgiven for imagining that, somewhere not-here, a lever in a great cosmic machine is waiting to drop.

Somewhere not-here, a sorcerer is gathering his ingredients and practising the Latin pronunciation of a spell.

Something like that. Something occulted and strange and many miles remote from Billy Ferretti and the chipped white mugs and the neon sign that says *Have a nice day!* above the menu in Suzy's All-American Diner. If anyone here feels its imminence, perhaps they turn a page of Saturday's free paper, or glance up the road with an eye out for disapproving neighbours, but more likely they don't. More likely, they feel nothing at all.

Suzanne Powell opened the Diner in 1989 with Hollywood sunsets in her eyes, with dreams that she'd head out there someday and sip milkshakes sitting blonde and hotpants-clad in a booth of cherry-red leather, drive a convertible on the scorching tarmac of a road where it never rained, meet a lifeguard who'd call her 'sweetheart' and kiss her on a beach in Los Angeles. She'd learn to cook like an American, too: fat, squidgy stacks of pancakes topped with pats of butter; golden-brown waffles scattered with powdered sugar and strawberry slices; meatloaf and damn fine cherry pie.

Suzanne never scraped together the money, and Suzy's All-American Diner has peeling pleather booths that might once have approximated cherry, but it serves beans on toast and fry-ups and tea and cake and jacket potatoes with a choice of five toppings.

Billy orders a full English, eggs sunny side up. It's that, scrambled, or a withering look and a semi-poached mess if you ask for anything more involved.

Suzanne retired eight years ago and spends every minute she can at the static caravan in the Gower. She'll be there now, sitting on the little blue foldaway couch with the telly turned to BBC One. Her daughter Lizzie (after Taylor, *not* Windsor, thank you very much) mans the counter, scowling in defiance at any passer-by who dares a reproachful look.

The TV above the till is her sole concession to the occasion, volume tuned to a low burble as the text ticker along the bottom of the screen breathlessly announces each step the coffin takes toward Westminster Abbey, each arrival, each royal blink or sneeze. Billy slides into his usual seat in the booth nearest the window, back to the glass and the bruise-dark cloud-face louring over the valley walls. Finds himself keeping half an eye on the telly even though he's determined not to care and distracts himself with the laminated menu card.

Some ballpoint-wielding local wit has defaced the dessert menu, which, in an uncharacteristic bout of imagination, Lizzie has divided into seven types of cake themed for the seven deadly sins. Cartoon devils with pitchforks wink from the margins.

LUST, exclaims the menu, in a font straight from one of the heavy metal T-shirts Billy's kid brother lives in (still, even though he's twenty-nine). *Three layers of moist and decadent chocolate cake filled with ganache and buttercream. Did you know chocolate was once considered an aphrodisiac?*

Beneath that, blue ballpoint ink:

Did you know it was once considered a medicine? Did you know the Maya drank it bitter?

Do you ever wonder why medicine must be vile, why we only sugar it for children, why we withhold the drip of softness and honey from those at destitution's door and wait to offer the bitter medicine until they have abased themselves like kicked dogs?

Do you watch your signing-on neighbours jealously for evidence of new phones? Do you read about girls of twenty trading sex for rent and think they should have managed their money better? Do you get home from your forty-grand job and tell yourself that, after such a long day, you deserve a little treat, so you pop to the shop and buy yourself a bar and don't think about the child labour that made it?

Did you know, Columbus or Cortés, chocolate has no origin story that isn't freighted with conquest?

Billy snorts at the looping copperplate, grandmother handwriting like a letter from a history book; at the childishly over-earnest outpouring, surely not meant for him. He's got no forty-grand job, that's for sure. Billy grew up above his grandparents' café, spent Saturdays washing dishes while his classmates played football and chatted up girls, and though at the time the promise of a birthright sounded like the clang of a cage door, when the red-and-white striped awning was torn down and the windows boarded up, something was wrenched out by the root from his chest and he fled to the Cardiff Arms and drank until he couldn't feel his face.

He works in a window factory now, where health and safety's a joke and the foreman'll get you any drug you want inside an hour. It pays the bills, and in a couple of months he might even be able to afford a new washing machine instead of lugging his laundry downhill to the butter-yellow nineties time-capsule of his parents' kitchen every Sunday.

So, yeah. Definitely not for him.

Somewhere, a mechanism clicks into place.

Somewhere, a sorcerer lights candles and sweeps dust from an altar with the palm of his venerable hand and is almost ready.

Billy's parents asked him over to watch the funeral. He demurred and claimed a headache, and now — though the streets are almost empty and Mam will no doubt be perched at respectful attention on the edge of her seat as the coffin processes toward its final resting place — he folds himself into the corner of the faded red booth like he's fifteen years old and smoking behind the houses.

Lizzie fetches his coffee: treacle-thick with two sugar packets at the side. A tablespoon's worth slops into the saucer as she sets it down carelessly, mind not on the TV and the funeral procession, nor the glinting sea and the great open spaces of America, but on the big white house she'll buy down near Cardiff when she gets rid of this place. It'll have to wait until Suzanne's gone, of course — it'd break the old girl's heart — but in Lizzie's head the big white house is a cathedral of dreams, high-ceilinged and so clean it glows when the sun climbs up past the hills in the morning; and once she lives in it her children will be grateful and her husband will wipe his piss off the toilet seat and the inside of her head will at last be serene and calm as a snow day.

The news drones on above the counter in respectful monotone, noting positions, military uniforms, medals, as though any of these things means anything outside its own arcane grammar. Billy stirs in both sugars, sips his coffee, and it is surely the caffeine and nothing else that makes his pulse tick up to an uncomfortable speed inside his throat, the sense of something waking creep down his spine.

GREED, reads the menu. *Millionaire's shortbread. Buttery biscuit topped with layers of velvety caramel and rich milk chocolate. Live like a lottery winner, just for one day.*

Have you ever seen a millionaire eat one of these things? Of course not, they're all on green juice cleanses and keto diets, not that you or I know what that's supposed to mean.

No, this is the kind of thing you throw into your trolley because it has a yellow discount sticker and still feel guilty about; the kind of thing you buy as an affordable bit of indulgence but end up shoving down your gullet on your smoke break to keep yourself going through the ache in your shoulders and the tired fuzz in your brain.

Wealth isn't written on the body, or anyway not the way we imagine it is. It's not the spilling-over flesh of a storybook villain, no — it's muscle tone and bright-eyed energy and skin dermaplaned into uninterrupted peachy smoothness. Or it is utter ordinariness, thinning hair and shabby clothing that cost more than your month's rent.

Greed, though. Greed is as universal as breath, and you'll never, never grasp a thing worth having.

There's a jarring electronic chime as the door opens. Billy's head turns involuntarily toward the sound; then he wishes he hadn't looked, because Ceri Rhys has walked in.

She wears sensible shoes now, the same slip-on Skechers as every mam with a toddler to run around after, but the glossy liquorice shine of her black hair is the same, and her sweet, dirty laugh and the way her jeans hug her long, taut thighs. Billy still remembers the dimples on the insides of her knees. He remembers the way she'd hang around the cafe waiting for him to finish his shift, drinking black coffee with chemical sweetener and reading — she was the only person he knew who had a favourite poet — or leaning against the wall outside, smoking with the practised insouciance of a tragic movie starlet.

He's not sure if he wants her to notice him.

It seems at first that she won't, but she turns to look out the window while Lizzie rings up her cup of tea and her gaze homes in on him with a sniper's precision. Billy raises one hand in weak greeting.

Her rubber soles creak on the lino tiles and she slips onto the bench seat opposite. 'Hiya. How's your mam?'

His mother always liked her; still pointedly mentions it any time they run into each other down the shops. Billy hunches forward over his coffee and tears at one of the spent sugar packets, fifteen years old and awkward again in her presence. 'Alright. Same old.' He jerks his head at the TV for a change of subject. 'Not watching it, then?'

Ceri gives the practised grimace common to every harried parent. 'Nah. Kids need their Disney and I needed out of the house, you know how it is,' she says, and pulls herself up short, wincing. 'Or you don't. Unless…?'

She trails off, hopefully, and Billy could make something up to soften her blunder, but she'd find out eventually and that would be worse, so he says nothing.

Ceri pulls herself inward, elbows tucked to her sides. They were sixteen when she got pregnant, and the earnest, untarnished optimism with which Billy insisted his parents would help out, they'd get married (get married!), they'd cope, felt like a lead weight round her ankle dragging her into cold and brackish water. She made him promise to tell no-one and as far she knows he never broke his vow. But after she got rid of it, he was cruel in small, mundane ways until she dumped him: forgetting a date to go to the pub with his mates; offering to walk another girl home. The pity she now feels for his inarticulate teenage pain is undeserved and unreasoning, and she resents it in a small, niggling way, like a hangnail not quite worth the sting of peeling it off.

'Well,' she says, 'plenty of fish in the sea.'

Billy answers with a smile that isn't, really, and looks at the table.

WRATH has Lizzie, or whatever aspiring wordsmith she recruited to write the menu, scraping the barrel. *Our blueberry muffins, bursting with fresh fruit, are handmade in small batches by local bakery Alex Huggins – that's why they're only available on Fridays and Saturdays. You'll be kicking yourself if you miss out!*

The really sad thing is, you actually might.

Think of the last time you got shirty with someone being paid sweet FA to answer your phone call or serve your coffee, or kicked a door, or called a stranger pushing a pram too slowly for your liking a stupid cow under your breath. How small an inconvenience was it? Are you so coddled, so cocooned in comfort that any intrusion, no matter how brief, feels like violence? So pricked all over with minor indignities that when you lash out at one, it's with the frustration of a thousand other pains?

Do you think it matters to the person on the other end?

31

Breakfast comes out without ceremony, slapped down in front of Billy with a judder and a terse, 'Sauce?' from Lizzie.

Ceri lifts an eyebrow, and Billy is suddenly, painfully conscious of the way his jeans pull over his belly and how he was all bony angles like Nicky Wire when they were together, back when he was fizzing up all over with sixteen-year-old vitality and hope. 'Brown, please,' he mumbles, and wishes he'd had plain toast.

Lizzie plonks the bottle of HP on the table, thinking still of her big white house, and Ceri draws out her cup of tea with tiny sips and counts the minutes she dares take before she goes back home, and Billy sets aside the paper napkin, valiantly picks up his knife and fork, and begins to separate the translucent rind of fat from the thick, acetaldehyde-pink slices of bacon. He's no longer hungry, not even a little, but a lifetime of being chided for waste galvanises his hands into mechanical motion: cut, chew, swallow.

Somewhere, a cog turns, throwing the machine into unstoppable motion.

Somewhere, a circle drawn in salt, corners called, air charged with magic.

Ceri's belly rumbles. Billy's split egg yolk puddles on his plate, that intense yellow that somehow always makes her think of blood. And at the same time, she thinks of the long gold afternoons of adolescence, and how the coffee and sucralose and Billy would fill her up with a nauseous fizzy excitement that made her feel like so much sparkling air, and like they knew each other completely and the knowing would shine on forever. It was so certain, so pure and clear, like nothing ever has been again.

She gulps her tea fast enough it scalds the roof of her mouth. 'Better go. Take care, Billy.'

Billy watches her leave. Should say something, probably,

but he has a mouthful of underdone hash brown and by the time he swallows the door has clunked shut behind her.

PRIDE: *Our lemon drizzle cake is Suzy's own family recipe, and if being proud of it is wrong, we don't want to be right. It's moist and golden, and we think it deserves a medal.*

Actually, a cake's a perfectly respectable thing to be proud of. Can't fault you on that one, Suzy. You spent time and skill making something, and somebody else enjoyed it. Same as making a table, or writing a song, or being really good at eating pussy.

It's the other shit I don't get. Being proud of what your parents did because they made enough money for you to skate along the surface of life without ever getting your feet wet. Of your metabolism or the size of your dick or the fact that you're six feet tall. Of being born on this wet, miserable Atlantic rock that by rights ought to be a sodden hinterland on the far edge of the continent but managed to make itself enough other people's problem, push enough tendrils into enough soft places of the world and suck them dry, that it still thinks it's the bright centre. Of being born in the Western part of it, as though position relative to Offa's Dyke makes you Nye Bevan or Shirley Bassey or fucking Merlin.

It'd be nice to think it's all on the way out, the flag-waving, the pomp. Look in the splintering mirror and ask, how long can it sustain itself? But the answer is, longer than you think. It's a self-perpetuating system, subsisting forever on its own shit.

These might hurt like death throes, but the ache is only an abscess waiting to burst. A little pain, a little mess, and then business as usual.

God save the bloody Queen.

Billy glances up guiltily at the TV set, as though his mother or Huw Edwards or the Navy guard in their identical uniforms like little Lego men might be reading over his shoulder. He's never got it, not really — the reverence, the way the coronation china sits alongside the match-day hatred — but it's part of him nonetheless and it leaps out under pressure, a leak in a water-bed.

But no: they've made it into the abbey now, walls the colour of old bone, ceiling arches grasping at the heavens like phalanges in a giants' ossuary. *The Lord is My Shepherd* dirges up from the assembled dignitaries. Billy's mam is probably sniffing into her hanky by now.

Billy's eggs are running into the baked beans. He cuts into sausage and the overdone casing crinkles and flakes like old paint. It all tastes of nothing, of rain, of *nothing*, and Billy can't stop shovelling it into his mouth.

In the old days, at funerals, they would eat the sins of the dead. The meal was bread and beer — austere, as if to make up for the rich and varied wrongs with which it was larded — and perhaps it, too, tasted of nothing, of rain, of nothing. There would be sixpence for the sin-eater afterward and he would walk away, avoided by all around him.

But this is not a funeral with bread and beer, and Billy Ferretti paid seven quid for his breakfast.

This is a nation burying its sins under sombre pantomime and Paddington Bear and the fearful hush of good manners, under a blanket of roses so thick it is choking on their perfume.

There will be no exchange across the coffin. There will be no acknowledgement that sin exists at all.

And if Lizzie feels it now, some charge in the air or some gulping anticipation low in the belly, she tells herself it's nothing and turns the TV up, and Billy keeps on chewing, swallows down sausage and wet grey mushrooms and tepid coffee like an automaton, powered by an electricity he does not understand.

The parts of that cosmic machine are moving now with silent, deadly precision.

The sorcerer is in full voice, his incantation reaching its climax where the candles will flare up in streams of fire and the shrieks of the spirits put his hair on end.

Billy keeps skimming the menu, not watching the telly, and by now the graffiti preacher has started to get bored, underwriting *ENVY* (salted caramel – everybody wants a piece!) with, *Why are you keeping up with the Joneses when the Joneses are going round in circles?* and *SLOTH* (carrot cake – it's not one of your five a day, but you can pretend!) with, *Wake up, get up, do SOMETHING before it's too late.* Here, the copperplate handwriting turns childishly big and round, like when Ceri wrote their names intertwined in a heart on a desk in the back of maths class and they couldn't stop laughing all the way through detention.

Outside, the clouds press close together like spectators at a hanging. Lizzie, despite the mild September air, puts on her spare cardigan.

Billy swallows the last of his toast and chases it with the cold dregs in his cup. The sediment of two sugars drags gritty and too sweet over the back of his tongue.

GLUTTONY, says the menu. *Our choc-chip cookies look small, but you can't have only one!*

Oh, just eat the fucking biscuits. It's not like it matters anyway.

Billy's knife and fork hit the plate with a clang.

Though Suzy's has never been known for the American generosity of its portions, he feels stretched out with all he has eaten, as though if he looks down the skin of his stomach will be balloon-thin and all his organs swimming about on display like aquarium fish.

On TV, the funeral service is ending. The image cuts back to the studio.

The sorcerer falls silent, waiting. The machine has completed its task.

Billy Ferretti heaves himself out of his seat and into the quiet. His joints ache like an eighty-year-old man's and his whole body throbs like a blister, straining-full with sin and bitter alchemy and a breakfast that was not even all that good.

He feels like the Michelin man, limbs ponderous, ground shaking with every step, like Godzilla coming to town to stomp the buildings into dust, but not a single person in Suzy's All-American Diner turns to look at him. Not even Lizzie, fumbling with the buttons of her cardigan and ignoring with fierce resolve the thing that no-one knows for sure is happening but that hangs ozone-sharp in the air nonetheless.

Denny Lewis has given up on the bus and gone home. Ceri's taillights are long vanished, and the street is so, so empty and the clouds press in on the silence like a bruise.

Billy puts one foot in front of the other. He can't feel them.

It's like he's piloting some great mechanical construct, moving body parts that aren't quite his any longer. He wonders, in a slow underwater kind of a way, if he's having a stroke.

And then.

Billy looks down, and the veins on the backs of his hands pulse the violent bleeding yellow of egg yolks, sunny side up.

He blinks and his eyes gum up with it, hot viscous tears running down his face.

His skin crackles and flakes with overcooked char.

There is sugar and bacon rind and bile on the back of his tongue, and his tongue is just meat and his muscles are lead and his breath is the drone of a funeral hymn, and the thrash of his terrified heart inside his ribcage is the clamour of a thousand buried sins that the thin membrane of his skin cannot contain.

The skin splits open along the backs of his arms. His teeth are smeared across his lips as though by an invisible punch.

The skinful of sins that was Billy Ferretti bursts open screaming, and not a single curtain twitches along the entire street.

This is how the machinery of power works: unseen, unremarked-upon, remote, even when it is bright red and shrieking in the middle of your very own street.

This is how the magic works: you know the words to the spell and you feel the devil's breath hot on the back of your neck, and you bargain with your eyes closed and tell yourself afterward that it was only a dream.

And nobody looks out of a window, and nobody steps into the street, until the clouds burst and the rain comes down in guillotine sheets and the last ectoplasmic wisps of Billy Ferretti wash into the gutters and the drains and are gone, gone, gone.

***

There will be a missing person report. A desultory police investigation.

Billy's mam will sit at home and marinate in formless fear, because the Rhondda is honeycombed with old tunnels and Billy could be careless, couldn't he? If she'd only asked him a third time to come around that day maybe he would have done, and whatever happened, wouldn't have.

And Ceri Rhys will wonder why she didn't pay more attention the last time she saw him, because he seemed fine, but that's what they always say about depressed people, isn't it? What cold river would you have to plunge into, what current would have to snatch you up, for your body never to be found?

On the anniversary of the last time he was seen — which is marked by Union flag bunting and solemn speeches, though not for Billy — they will meet in Suzy's All-American Diner for tea and cake.

The graffitied menu will have been thrown out by then, of course, but they'll smile faintly at the cartoon devils as they exchange memories and dissect once again the junctures when they might have made a difference, might have stopped — well. Whatever happened.

There will be moments when they cry. There will be moments when they hold hands and talk about the good times, because it's not fair to remember him only as an unanswered question.

They will both agree that the police are useless, that everything is these days, but nothing can be done about it. It's the way things are. The machine is so big and they are so small.

They will trail off when they run out of memories and watch the tribute speeches on TV, grateful to be distracted, absorbed into something bigger than their own pain.

And when they step out into the rain they will feel better, clean, weightless, as though they have eaten only light and joy.

We Shall All Be Changed

Satterday Shaw

Mrs Williams's head rests on the bank as if she's resting on a pillow. Her eyes are open. She must be dead because she's so completely stiff and still. Except for her trouser leg, which ripples in the current. She's lying half in and half out of the water. She looks like she's made of plastic, not pinky-orange plastic like a doll but sort of white, almost see-through, like a food container.

Gloria wonders whether cells from a dead body would look different under her Christmas microscope to cells from somebody alive. But organelles move even in a thin layer of onion skin so bacteria and stuff probably move in cells from a dead person. No internet in the woods. She'll Google it when she gets home.

Gloria goes to St John Ambulance on Mondays to learn what to do in an emergency. She squats down, careful not to let water flow in over the tops of her wellies, and lifts Mrs Williams's hand even though she must be dead. No pulse at the wrist. Just in case, Gloria slides her own hand under the old woman's mac and the neck of her jumper. The wool clings to Gloria's fingers, cold and wet. No heartbeat. The other thing she ought to do is hold a mirror above Mrs Williams's mouth to see if breath will cloud the surface but of course she hasn't got a mirror with her.

Mrs Williams doesn't look dressed for the woods. She's

wearing a towny white mac, trousers not jeans, and shoes rather than boots.

Gloria sits on the bank and holds the dead woman's hand for a while in case she feels lonely. Mrs Williams's fingers are white on top but dark underneath like she's been picking blackberries, only it's not the right time of year for blackberries.

Dead reeds from last year lie flat all around. New green reeds are shooting up in between. Something plops into the water behind them. A kingfisher flashes across the weir.

Gloria doesn't know how she feels. That's one reason she likes science. It's easier to say how things are.

She knows that everything is alive. The birds that perch on twigs and sing about it all. The cat that twitches after the birds. The hedge where birds weave their nests, which sends out crazy shoots as the days grow longer and lighter.

And then there's death, which grown-ups don't like to talk about. Most death doesn't last long. Life starts up again, like trees, or invades death and feeds off it like flies laying eggs in a blackbird in the ditch, like magpies pecking out its eyes.

Grown-ups don't leave dead things lying around for life to feed off. When Gloria's gerbil Hammy died, Mam tucked him into cotton wool in a big matchbox and helped her to bury him at the back of the flowerbed and even Madge came out and stood with her eyes shut for a minute while Gloria said a prayer. The matchbox would make it harder for maggots or next door's cat or anyone to eat him.

When Taid died they wouldn't even let Gloria go to the funeral. She was only little.

It's confusing, because in another way death lasts forever. Hammy's never coming back and neither is Taid. He will never drum his fingers on the table, little finger first and index finger last, so fast it sounds like a galloping horse's hoofs. Gloria used to practise when she was about six but she could never do it in the right order.

Because grown-ups feel so uncomfortable with death, Gloria decides not to tell anyone about Mrs Williams.

Gloria starts to shiver sitting still and her feet hurt.

The clouds begin to change colour so she looks at the time on her phone. It's getting late. Mam insists she bring the phone when she goes out on her own because there are a few weirdos in the woods and Gloria's got to dial 999 if a man talks to her. Madge says Gloria is pure weird because every other eleven-year-old girl is desperate for her own phone. Gloria slips among the trees and hides whenever she sees anyone at all.

She sets off home. She doesn't say goodbye because Mrs Williams is dead.

Her mam says, 'Wash your hands,' and then, 'That's not two minutes.' Madge is out. She always goes out on Friday evenings except during lockdown. Gloria's mam and dad are fussing around the baby. The baby's name is Philomena but everyone calls her Philly except for Madge, who calls her Creamcheese. Philly is nearly two weeks old.

While they eat lentil shepherd's pie Gloria can hear a helicopter whopping overhead.

'Eat up, Gloria,' her dad says. 'It's your favourite.'

'Have you been eating sweets?' her mam asks.

Gloria keeps chewing but the carrots stick in her throat. She forces herself to swallow a few mouthfuls. After supper she's sick down the toilet. Her mam tucks her into bed.

The helicopter sounds noisier upstairs. It makes a roaring growling sound. It throbs like in a war film so that Gloria imagines that a war has started.

The noise approaches and then recedes. It fades into silence

41

and returns, like a thunderstorm. Gloria worries about how much fuel the helicopter must be using. Petrol and diesel are as bad as plastic. Gloria wants to travel in a wind-powered sailing ship, like Greta Thunberg. She doesn't want the earth to be covered in plastic with no bees to pollinate the fruit. It makes her feel scared to think about it.

Finally, the racket stops and everything goes quiet. The baby doesn't cry. Gloria doesn't hear Madge come in.

On Saturday morning Gloria's parents ask her to stay at home with Philly while they do the supermarket shop. The baby sleeps in her cot, swaddled in a sheet under a blanket. Gloria thought wrapping her tight like that must be cruel until she realised that it made the baby feel safe after being tucked up inside their mam's body. Philly is a good example of new life that is weak and at the same time powerful like a bud that forces its way through stones. The baby can't speak, dress or feed herself but manages to boss the entire family, except for Madge of course.

Madge slouches into the kitchen while Gloria is giving Philly a bottle. She grabs the Coco Pops, a bowl and the milk carton and sits down at the table. She stares at Gloria from her head to her feet and back up again and says, 'Weirdo.'

'Fat bum.' The word *fat* can always upset her big sister.

In the afternoon, her mam and dad allow Gloria to go out even though she was sick the evening before. Because she managed to eat lunch without vomiting, because she helped with the baby, and because Lowri Hopkins from down the street knocked for her and her parents want Gloria to make friends. They expect her to spend time with another girl because that girl is exactly the same age and is in the same class at school. They probably wouldn't expect a grown-up to be friends for those reasons.

The girls don't walk along the river but up the lane to the West Wood. They play forts in a ruined house, abandoned after chemicals from the mine poisoned its water supply.

Mrs Williams's son strides past in the company of some other grown-ups. Gloria and Lowri squat behind half a wall coated with shaggy green moss. 'They're looking for Mrs Williams,' Lowri whispers. 'She's gone missing. The helicopter was out searching last night.'

Gloria feels uncertain what to do. If Mrs Williams were still alive, she'd run out and tell the son where his mam is. She would have phoned 999 and told somebody the day before. But she's not wrong. Grown-ups hate talking about death.

She doesn't want to upset anybody. She doesn't want to get into trouble. She doesn't want a *fuss*.

'They're Roman soldiers. They have strength in numbers and military training,' she whispers back to Lowri. 'If they capture us, they'll force us to fight tigers in the Colosseum.'

'They'll send us to a fate worse than death.'

What could that be, a fate worse than death?

The girls crouch on a carpet of leaves in a corner of the old kitchen. Gloria knows that it used to be the kitchen because if she adjusts her sight she can see a transparent woman lifting a kettle from the fireplace and pouring water into a teapot.

On Sunday it rains. Gloria finishes her homework. She tries to Google *do cells from living bodies move more than cells from dead bodies?* but she can't find any clear answers. She eats her dinner without being sick so her mam lets her go out as long as she carries her phone and wears her waterproofs. She says no when her dad suggests that she take next door's dog, because she wants to visit Mrs Williams and feels worried that Samson might start chewing the corpse. Even though Mrs Williams is dead, which means it would be part of the food chain for a carnivore to eat her and absorb her nutrients, Gloria doesn't want to observe this particular process. She's desperate to be a scientist when she grows up and her ambition requires unflinching scrutiny, but there are limits.

In Year 4 when they did food chains, Lowri was a lettuce leaf but Gloria had to be a slug and then Cian Jones was a really annoying bird who kept pecking Gloria's tummy with stiff fingers.

On the telegraph pole at the end of the street there's a notice with a photograph of Mrs Williams. *Missing Woman*, it says, and asks anyone with knowledge of her movements to contact the police.

An outsize police van has parked near the bridge. Gloria will lead them to Mrs Williams. She'll be a hero and get a medal. Her mam and dad will feel proud of her and Madge will want to sit with her on the bus.

As Gloria crosses the road to tell the police where the missing woman is, a policeman and policewoman unload a gigantic bay horse. Then they lead a black horse with a white forehead down the ramp. They seem so busy that Gloria wobbles and retreats.

She walks for nearly an hour through Coed Felin. The last half mile, after the pylons, is only a hedgehog path where she has to duck under bushes. The rain has stopped but branches drip down her neck.

She wonders whether Mrs Williams has changed or whether anything has chewed at her. But she's got to visit in case the dead woman may be lonely. Last night she could hear her parents murmuring. She deciphered her dad saying, 'Pat Williams,' her mam saying, 'lonely' and her dad saying, 'benefits stopped.'

Friday, Saturday, Sunday. It's the third day. On the third day Jesus rose again from the dead and ascended into heaven. Maybe Mrs Williams has risen again, or the rain has washed her away.

But Gloria can see the woman's mac. Neither her face nor her mac looks so white anymore. Her skin has turned a funny colour and only dark patches remain where her eyes used to be.

Gloria glances away immediately. She doesn't want to see.

She trips over a root and stumbles into the edge of the river where she treads on the loose flap of Mrs Williams's trousers.

A small brown eel shoots out of the submerged trouser leg and vanishes into the water. Gloria knows that the European eel feeds on invertebrates such as insect larvae, which means the eel was hiding rather than eating any part of Mrs Williams. But it still makes her feel as though all the blood flowing through her veins has developed prickles.

Her mouth floods with saliva. She leans forward to avoid the dead woman's legs and vomits into the water. Her Sunday dinner spews out of her mouth, fragments in a yellow liquid even though the meal had nothing yellow in it. The vomit burns Gloria's throat. It blends with the river where it cascades over the edge of the weir.

Water trickles into one of Gloria's wellies. She lurches back onto the bank and crouches on the wet reeds.

She can't hold the old woman's hand. It's beyond her.

Everything is lifeless. No life in the stones, the water or the pale clouds. No life in the pale reeds or the dripping trees. The holly tree looms black and dead. The sky spreads out white and dead. Everything is dead and ominous.

Mrs Williams is dead and everything is wrong and Gloria has got it all wrong and she doesn't know what to do.

It's impossible to hold Mrs Williams's hand so instead

Gloria talks to her. 'Mrs Williams — Pat,' she mutters, and then clears her throat and tries to speak more clearly. 'That was a European eel, probably a male because it was quite small. Or it could have been a young female. European eels lead amazing lives! Every single one of them begins like a transparent leaf in the Sargasso Sea. That sea is in the middle of the Atlantic Ocean and is called after a kind of seaweed that floats on the surface. So anyway, the larvae drift along the Gulf Stream until they reach a coastline and then they change into baby eels — elvers — and they go on adventures into rivers and they can do anything, climb waterfalls, or swim up steep rock faces —'

At that moment the sun shines through the clouds and lights Mrs Williams's mac, trousers and shoes. The light makes everything glisten: the weir, the trees and the ruined mill where the mill stream used to run.

Birds start to sing as though competing in a TV talent competition. The change is so extraordinary that Gloria expects Mrs Williams to rise again or some transparent approximation of her spirit to shimmer out of her body and float up into heaven.

Gloria fixes her gaze on the area around Mrs Williams's heart in order to avoid catching sight of her face.

She waits for something to happen.

The sun vanishes behind clouds. The chill seeps from the ground into Gloria's bottom and her wet foot feels freezing. She's shivering. The mile or so back to the village stretches in her thoughts until it becomes too far.

She fumbles the phone from her pocket and finds her sister's number. No internet here in the woods but she's got signal.

'Madonna, where are you?'

Gloria waits for Madge at the bus stop.

'What's up, *sosej*?' Madge asks as soon as the bus has roared away. She says it with a fake Welsh accent. 'You're as white as a skellington.'

Gloria blurts out everything about knowing where Mrs Williams is and not wanting to tell their parents or the police. Not knowing what to do.

'You're right not to tell the zombies,' which is what Madge calls their mam and dad since the baby was born. 'And you're right not to tell the police. They might think she's been murdered and you're the murderer. What we need is an anonymous phone call... if they haven't found her by tomorrow. There's a phone box near my school. Leave it to me.'

When they arrive home, Madge makes hot chocolate and she and Gloria slump on the sofa to watch reruns of *16 and Pregnant* because there's nothing else on.

'Forty and pregnant is worse, for bollocks' sake,' Madge says. But she lets Gloria have the comfortable end and lifts Gloria's feet onto her lap.

On Monday morning Mam says Gloria looks peaky and places a hand on her forehead.

'Mam, can I go back to bed?' Gloria asks.

'Creep,' says Madge.

'Punk.'

'Eat some breakfast first,' their mam says.

Gloria rests in bed all morning with the radio on. She eats tomato soup for lunch downstairs with her mam and then gets dressed.

Her mam lets her push Philly along the pavement in her pram while she catches up with emails even though she's supposed to be off work.

As Gloria and the baby approach the bridge, a police van

that has MARINE UNIT on the side parks next to the verge. Two men in waterproofs shuffle their arms into life jackets. They unload an orange inflatable dinghy from the trailer, wrestle it into the water and fix an outboard motor on the back.

Gloria presses down on the handle of the pram to turn it. She pushes Philly home.

All the houses in their street have small yards and kitchen doors that are the front doors because they were built for miners who did dirty work and needed a wash on their way inside.

Mrs Williams lives on the other side of the main road in one of the semis. Lived.

Gloria cuddles the sleeping baby in her arms while she watches a DVD. When Philly wakes and grizzles, Gloria gives her to Mam to feed. 'I'll change her nappy as long as she hasn't done a poo,' she tells her mam.

Philly cries when Gloria folds her legs into her sleepsuit. Gloria can hear an echo to her mewling as if, somewhere, some transparent other baby is crying too but she concentrates on listening to her own little sister.

After the baby's fastened back into her sleepsuit she smiles at Gloria. Gloria carries her into the kitchen to tell her mam, who glances up from her laptop.

'She *does* smile, doesn't she? People say babies can't smile till they're six weeks old, but it's not true.'

Madge slams in after school. Gloria stops herself from asking about anonymous phone calls and Madge doesn't say anything. Gloria can't go to St John Ambulance because she's been poorly.

On Tuesday Gloria goes back to school. She walks to the bus stop with Lowri Hopkins. Madge hurries ahead, ignoring them.

Lowri asks, 'Didn't you know? They found Mrs Williams yesterday afternoon down near the mill. In the river. She was *dead*.' She says it as if Gloria must be ignorant for not knowing and as if the event is somehow exciting rather than sad and terrible.

'That's really sad,' Gloria says. She wants to change the subject. 'Anyway, what are you going to do your science project on?'

She starts to tell Lowri about the life cycle of the European eel and how the larvae drift and swim for three thousand miles to reach their very own river.

The Pier

Emma Moyle

The sixth of April is the third day in a stretch of unseasonably warm weather for southern England. Shops in the seaside resort are already selling out of summer stock, and beach bars and restaurants are busy in the lengthening evenings. The pier prepares for another unexpected windfall of a day this early in the season. Slot machines are wiped down, fired up, and brightly-painted carriages on vertiginous structures run through their safety checks. One of the big water rides has developed a problem and an engineer is called out.

Jac Lewis is late for his shift. Arriving at 9:18am, looking rather worse for wear after early celebrations for his twenty-third birthday the night before, he makes for the staff lockers in the dingier part of the main amusement arcade. He knows he needs to avoid at least two of his female colleagues, but he's not entirely sure just how bad things got last night. He's fairly positive that he hasn't made any headway with Sugar. His supervisor catches a fleeting glimpse of stubble and a red shirt that obviously is sleep-creased. She has no time to remonstrate with him right now – she'll catch him later. Everyone else knows that she has a soft spot for Jac and that he's allowed to get away with black nail varnish and piercings that would see any other employee being asked to leave. Jac knows this; he's not above turning it to his advantage. He sees Sugar already in place at the token kiosk and tries out a sheepish grin. He is pointedly ignored.

At 11:03am, forty-three-year-old Judith Smith arrives at the entrance to the pier with her three-year-old daughter, Tabby. They pass in front of the security cameras, Tabby skipping with anticipation. Judith's already tired and deliberating on the best way to string out activities as cheaply as possible until she can go home and put *Cbeebies* on. Caught out by the weather, for surely no one would expect this to last, Judith is already regretting the coats and large bag she will have to lug around for the next few hours. She wishes that it wasn't always just the two of them, that Daddy might be able to take more time off from work to be there, to bloody well help carry things at the very least. She decides that the day will be far more successful if she buys a latte right now; she and her daughter find a small table and she buys Tabby a snack, just so she has five minutes of silence in which to drink her coffee. Two men manoeuvre a huge mirror ball past them on a trolley. Judith muses idly about how its multi-faceted surface reflects but doesn't actually allow you to see a reflection. Probably best – it's a while since she's taken a good look at herself. She takes a photo of her coffee and posts it, taking a minute or two to compose a wry caption.

Two minutes after Judith and Tabby have sat down at their table, Siobhan Johnson, a pretty woman in her late twenties, is captured by the security cameras pushing her son onto the pier in his buggy. She is accompanied by a man, her older brother, a hulking man of indeterminate age for an onlooker. He is seen taking a proprietorial concern over his sister's day out, making a good deal of fuss over his nephew, and pointing out the swooping seagulls which have caught the child's attention. The family of three pass Judith and Tabby at their table. Siobhan's sunglasses reflect the pier and the doughnut stand as she passes, and Judith recognises another mother's attempt to hide the inevitable exhaustion. Judith has given up putting on make-up for the time being and is still wearing clothes she wore before Tabby was born. Siobhan, on the other hand, is obviously still aware of what passes for current style, even if she has little money and depends on the discount stores for any new clothes. Her make-up is flawless, and not for the first time in recent months, Judith feels a stab of envy at those women who know how to do such things. While she thinks this over, Siobhan, her brother and the child move past and are lost in the already crowded promenade.

At 11:21am, the cameras record a man in a heavy woollen jacket and dark glasses entering the pier. He is clean-shaven, conventionally good-looking, and leans forward slightly into his walk, placing his weight on the balls of his feet. He is seen glancing around. The only thing that is perhaps noteworthy is that he is on his own, that he isn't being pulled along by a child, or isn't arm in arm with someone. But then there are many solitary visitors to the pier who come for the machines, the games in the darkness of the main arcade, the thrill of an unlikely win to pass the time.

The day is getting steadily warmer, even at this early hour, and the ice cream kiosk is already running out of cones. The unseasonal temperature is aggravating Jac's headache and he desperately needs water. He's been put on the carousel as an act of kindness by his supervisor; he's sweating already and manning this ride means he can stand in the shade of the nearby fun-house. All he has to do is collect tokens and make sure everyone is seated before he starts the machinery up. He's supposed to run a thorough safety check each time. Siobhan's brother secures his arms around her small son as they sit expectantly together on a lion frozen in mid-roar. Her son is laughing up at his uncle and Siobhan waves madly as soon as they slowly move past her. She'll look up in time for them coming round again. She twitches in her bag for her phone, frowning in the sun as she scrolls. Then, keeping one hand on the pushchair, she puts away her phone and gazes around the pier. She seems briefly interested by the young man who is operating the ride but clearly wishing he was elsewhere. Jac sees her looking at him and he stares back, something asserting itself despite the hangover. She's attractive. He knows what she's thinking: he isn't her type – she would prefer them clean-cut – but many of her friends would find him fit. They both look away at the same time.

By half past twelve, Tabby and Judith are sitting down in the restaurant on the pier. If she'd been alone, Judith would have occupied one of the blue and white striped deckchairs and got out a book. But there's no book in her large bag and there are still hours to kill. Tabby is colouring in a paper placemat with the complementary crayons and Judith is watching people. Better to take an interest in people in the real world, she reminds herself, than to do it scrolling through updates. Outside, crowds continue to stream past at a steady rate. A toddler is screaming. A group of young men are heading down to the end, already laughing at the idea of getting soaked on the log flume. A young man in a dark jacket and shades has been asked to get rid of his cigarette by a security guard and has thrown it into the sea with a grimace. Judith wonders if the heat is getting to him – he should take off that heavy jacket. Now he checks his phone. A family of four, the teenage boys wearing football tops in colours Judith doesn't recognise, are taking turns to smile through the cut-out face holes on a board of jolly, wobbly cartoon bodies whilst their mother laughs and takes photos to remember their day out. An employee moves along the pier, wiping down all the safety notices. It is dangerous and forbidden to jump off the pier.

After lunch, Judith and Tabby return to the small and suitably tame children's rollercoaster. Judith is able to lean her bag and the coats against the wooden railing as she watches her daughter travel slowly round and round in a toy police car. Nearby, older riders are screaming their way round a terrifying series of high-speed corkscrews and plunges. Judith shudders at the idea of such desired fear. Did she ever have the nerve, when she was younger, to go on such things? She tries to avoid checking her phone for new notifications – it's not good for Tabby to see her mother constantly scrolling through social media sites, and god knows the rolling news is just one violent nightmare after another. It feels good to lay everything down and stand in the sun. She sees the young mother with the impeccable make-up helping her son climb into one of the cars. His uncle is taking photos of the boy on his phone and trying to get the child to look towards him. As the woman returns to the man's side, Judith overhears her say he 'can't put it on Facebook, remember'. Judith thinks she understands this – she herself has become uncomfortable at the idea that Tabby's face might be liked by friends and seen by others. You just have to be so careful. Cameras checked in the coming days will show that the man with the jacket and shades, standing some way off, is watching the ride closely.

Twenty minutes later, Judith can feel her neck getting burnt and convinces Tabby that it would be good to move onto the bouncy castle. Why don't they have more coffee kiosks down this end of the pier? The young man now manning the bouncy castle is swigging from a bottle of water and managing to look pale under an early tan and quite a lot of stubble. Judith is amused by his brusque manner with the small children careering around inside the inflated castle; there's no attempt to soften his manner when he calls the end of a time slot. Judith seeks a sliver of shade at the side and finds herself next to the young employee, a lopsided badge on his red top identifying him as 'Jack'. It's a good name for him, she decides, for like others before her, she sees something piratical in his jet-black hair, stubble and silver earring. She imagines it's a studied look and she feels a warmth towards the young man who has perhaps sought adventures and found himself in a kids' fairground instead. He certainly doesn't fit here. For want of anything better to do, she thinks, he strikes up conversation with her. She's amused that he's so bored that he will grope around for something to say to a woman her age. But she's bored too and manages to keep the conversation afloat, finding out that he's lived here for two years, would like to go to Australia to try out the surf, and that today is his twenty-third birthday. His Welsh accent is still strong and he misses the proper beaches back home. She recognises in him the boys she went to school with, the boys who all wanted to get out and make a grand gesture, for whom a small Welsh town was not enough. He tells her that he's only doing this job whilst he saves up, and that *Point Break* is his favourite film, even if, and she stifles a smile at this, it is quite old now. All the time he's talking to her, Judith notes that his eyes keep flicking back to a female employee behind her at the next ride.

After a gulp of water, Tabby is on the bouncy castle again, allowing Judith another ten precious minutes to stand and look out to sea. This is the way to get through the day. She moves to the railing and this gives her an excellent view of the rest of the pier. Two men atop the main amusement arcade are coaxing the giant mirror ball back into action. Slowly, it begins to revolve, sending small darts of light out into the bright sky. Judith feels a moment of unalloyed pleasure, here in the sun, with the garish pier doing what it does best. It is from here, in this moment of calm that she is always looking for, that she is witness to the events now unfolding further up the promenade.

The young family she's spotted on her rounds are now halfway up the pier, but this time they have been joined by the man in the dark jacket. He seems agitated, is shouting, gesturing forcefully at the uncle. Judith makes out something about 'how would she like it?'. The young woman has picked the child up and is looking around her fearfully, but the man and his anger are blocking the way off the pier. She has taken off her sunglasses and those near her later say they could see an old bruise near the eye socket. In the shock of a single moment, the young man grabs for the child, pulling him out of his mother's arms forcefully. The child is crying, and it looks as though the man makes a brief attempt to soothe him. This doesn't work and so the man is shouting again, backing away, and aghast onlookers are learning that this is the child's father, that he has rights too. And that he isn't going to let that bitch treat him like this. As the child's uncle lunges for the boy, the father turns sharply towards the sea and, seemingly without hesitation, holds his son over the low railing, high over the sea below. Everything, everyone stops. The father's face is twisted as he turns to the boy's mother, challenging her with this most terrible of gambles. She is breathing raggedly, imploring her husband to listen to her. The uncle has his arms outstretched, muttering words to soothe his distraught nephew. A circle has gathered around the four central figures in this stand-off. A woman is on her phone, shrieking for assistance. Judith is horrified to see another man filming the event on his phone. She finds herself calculating the depth of the water, the time it might take her to swim to the spot beneath the child if he fell, if he were dropped. Where are the steps? What would she do with Tabby? To her relief, she sees that two men have broken away from a gathering crowd on the shingle beach and have waded into the waves, unseen by the protagonists on the pier's edge. It would still be a drop of what, forty feet? There is the distant wailing of a siren. It's the arrival of two burly security men, talking into their radios, that distracts the man holding the child above the sea and his eyes flash manically from one to the other. This development seems to galvanise the uncle. Making a grab for his nephew, he manages to seize hold of the boy's left ankle. Enraged, the father swings round, loosening his grip on the boy, but the uncle hangs on and the child is there, dangling above the drop. From seemingly nowhere, a spiky-haired employee has charged into the space around the family and thrown an arm around the father's neck, the momentum causing him to lose his balance. Judith just has time to recognise the figure of Jac as he and the father seem to pause briefly before plunging over the side of the pier in a tangled struggle. The child has been pulled back over the railings and is being held tightly by his mother. He is safe and will not remember this day himself. Another child will reveal it all at school when he is much older. His uncle collapses onto the boards, and he is held gently by a stranger who has knelt beside him, her teenage boys in their football kits helplessly standing by. Judith feels sick and it is with some difficulty that she tears her eyes away to look down into the sea. The two swimmers from the beach have reached Jac and the other man, are dragging them back towards the shore where police officers have arrived.

The pier closes for business that day at 14:05, with police taking statements from witnesses whilst seagulls swoop and a young woman called Sugar is overtaken by a feeling of loss she could never have expected. Those who had been on rides, who had not seen the event itself, are perplexed as to why they're being asked to leave the pier, why barriers on rides are closing early. A team of red-shirted employees moves slowly down the promenade, firmly ushering the more belligerent visitors away. The staff are grim-faced. After waiting her turn, Judith gives a witness statement to a young police officer. She is unable to recall the exact sequence of events and now isn't sure when she saw the young family and at which ride. The things that have stuck in her head are the light glancing off the pier's glitter ball as the struggle unfolded and Jac's desire to travel. She tells the police officer that they came from nearby Welsh towns and then feels embarrassed at the pointlessness of such information. She is asked if she has any photos or film on her phone which may be useful. She doesn't. Later, Judith takes her daughter to a nearby ice cream parlour and weeps quietly, turning her head away, whilst Tabby spoons ice cream from a large fluted bowl. As far as her child is concerned, this has been a very good day indeed.

In the days ahead, Judith will scour online news reports, needing to retain some connection to the event and the people involved. She wishes she had been a more reliable witness. She will learn that Alex Johnson, 32, is now in custody and will face charges brought by his estranged wife. His broken leg will mend. He will say he only wanted to frighten his wife, to make her see sense. Judith will learn that Jac Lewis, young insouciant Jac from south Wales who did so want to impress himself on those around him, Jac with serious spinal injuries and red blood slipping from his mouth, is pronounced dead at 13:52, just under fourteen hours into his twenty-third birthday. Jac will be hailed a hero in the local paper, even if they have got his name wrong; he will get a brief mention on the national news. In a meeting away from the eyes of the press, Siobhan Johnson will tell his mother that he saved her boy's life. The picture chosen by his mother shows an angular seventeen-year-old boy in a school jumper, with short brown hair and pimples round his mouth. His eyes are already looking elsewhere.

The pier's owner debates investing in prevention strategies which will make such tragedies less likely. More security cameras will be installed. In dreams, Judith will see an image of a child at the railings. Sometimes it is Tabby who is there, facing the sea. Always, it is Jac, seen from a variety of often improbable perspectives, who is falling, his long limbs tumbling before he hits the shallow surf.

The Nick of Time

Dan Williams

He was thinking about the view laid out beyond the chipped and grimy windscreen and she was thinking about cutting. For Len the future was a project half started and sometimes picked up; for Maggie it was cutting, slicing, nicking. So many things to do back at the cottage: a dinner to prepare, dogs to feed, feral cats that she liked to think loved her. And the wood. Most of all, the wood. The wood in the shed. Cutting, slicing, nicking.

The van, laden with the weight of boxes they had bought, belched along the empty lanes, the town now twenty miles behind them. Weaved into the scrape and rattle of the engine drifted the faint melody of a dozen old mantel clocks; inconsistent harmonies bumped out to the inconsistent rhythm of the road.

Maggie looked out of the passenger window and smiled. The view had opened up as they crested the hill and revealed, like the opening of a curtain, a world of shades and layers. A world of colours that pastelled into the distance and faded to a grey darker by a tint than the one before. The Giant's Chair brooding in the misty distance. Closer, all the greens of the world assembled and splashed about the trees across the valley. Clouds were gathering too far to worry about: here the sun shone as it should in the middle of May.

But it wasn't the view that Maggie was smiling at.

***

Len had his attention on the road and silently prayed for the rusted old shed to make it home with the treasure. *Come on Beauty*, he might have been saying to himself, *just get us home this one more time and I'll see to you*. It was an old prayer.

He wouldn't see to the van, though. Had been praying the same prayer at the same place every second Thursday in the month for as many months as Maggie could remember since moving here. As was so often the case with Len, he always somehow made it home.

He didn't notice that his newest wife was smiling as she gazed out of the window, but if he had he would have been sure that it was because of how lucky they both were to have escaped from their pasts: any woman would be happy to live such a life with such a man. With him. Len. What a gift.

He leaned over. Over the pile of unfinished lunch and crumpled invoices to touch her knee: *Lovely, this,* he said.

She jumped a little. Not enough so that he would notice. He rarely noticed that sort of thing. But enough to shock her back to her senses; to make her realise that she had drifted again. She scolded herself secretly before she turned, smiled and whispered:

So beautiful.

The rhythm of the road and her own thoughts had hypnotised her after the long day, making her drop her guard a little. It wasn't the trees or the garish yellow of the fields. It certainly wasn't the isolation of the little place they were heading back to or the thankless hens and needy cats and dogs that would love her briefly until they were sated. Like he would when they (if they ever) got there. Cutting. She needed to be home, cutting.

Maggie had been lost. Lost even beyond her thoughts of all the cutting she needed to do. Only for a moment or two, but veritably lost in the whisper of a deeper thought from another time in a different century when her clock had hardly thought of starting to tick, and kids, let alone grandkids, were someone else's idea. When only marriage was a worthy dream and it was Colin, not Len, who was driving the car. A real car. An Austin, maybe. Or a Volvo? Something solid. It wasn't the tops of the trees that she was searching for as they flashed by, nor distant fields. It was the heights of the tall city buildings and the lights of the busy roads that floated in front of her eyes.

A marriage on the horizon and a trip to town for, what now? Music, maybe. A concert. Drinks with friends and laughter and beautiful clothes and clean skin. *His* hand on her thigh as they drove home. Every beat of her heart splashed across her chest so that she was sure Len would see it.

But it wasn't Colin's hand on her thigh and the hot machine smell wasn't that of the city but of a struggling engine and a burning clutch.

She turned from the window and smiled, remembering that this was a marriage which they'd all laughed at when they went and did it. *Old fools*, that's what she'd imagined them saying, though nobody ever did to their faces. She had his hand in both of hers and held it there, recapturing the hope of the moment. Thinking of the jobs she had to do.

So you think we've done ok today then, love? she said.

It was the perfect question.

There's some beauties in that one box. I knew there was. Whittington chime, one of them. That's unusual. Not like your Big Ben. Whittington, as in Dick. Like the cat.

His eyes widened as he thought of the boxes piled in the back.

That one's worth a fortune. I knew the other fellas hadn't seen it. Made sure.

Here he paused, waiting for her to urge him on as she always did. When she said nothing, he said:

You know what I did? I used some of those dusters and covered her up at viewing so she was hidden at the bottom. So's nobody'd see her.

Maggie smiled and slid one of her hands from his so that she could lean over and rub at the ketchup stain on Len's chest.

That's naughty, she said. Then: *This'll never come out, you know.*

Len clicked his tongue, remembered standing at the burger van outside the market in his white football shirt, grinning at the Welshmen huddled over photostat lists of lots. From time to time they would look up at this imposter, his shirt worn just to wind them up. They favoured the dragon over the lions: red over white. When they had smiled at him today, Len had thought that he'd finally been accepted into the tough world of the Pont-Newydd bric-a-brac auction house. Until Maggie had stepped forward with the baby-wipe. His face burned thinking about it. The red stain oozing down the white shirt.

Len sighed, briefly melancholic.

Still, got them clocks. Those gits didn't.

Maggie patted his hand then gazed dreamily again out of the window, the emptiness of the road and the landscape that went on forever to nothing more than a darkening weight of grey. Of Colin and of nicking, slicing, cutting.

She thought of her old lovers, of her children and of their children in a way that Len never seemed to think of his. She supposed he kept his mind busy with the stuff; the stuff that they carted back to the old barn every other Thursday; stuff that he spent his time looking through and sorting into piles. Piling and listing while she cut and sliced and nicked.

More and more weight. Piling and listing and valuing, but never selling. Accumulating as the timbers of the old place groaned beneath the burden.

She supposed she was bored, that's what it came down to. Bored of backwards and forwards on the same empty roads with no towns. Bored of loading and unloading hefty lots up creaking stairs into what used to be a hayloft.

And the routine, Jesus, she hated it. The trip, the stupid loads, the lugging *up*stairs and never *down*stairs. And the other bits, too. The stupid hens at feeding time and the stupid cats and the stupider dogs. And Len. Loving her when they wanted her. She was bored of the constant slicing of bread and meat and stinking food from tins in the silent kitchen, of the chopping and cutting of wood in the chill of the barn while he mooched and muttered high above.

When was the last time she had gone out? When was the last time she had put on real clothes and worn perfume? Worn shoes instead of wellingtons and been waited on? Listened to real people and real music? She even longed to feel the throb of the traffic of a real town. That would be life at least.

In the end they had walked away with fifteen lots. Fifteen piles of boxes and sacks of miscellany ranging from baby clothes to cleaning products and everything else in between. All bits and pieces that weren't worthy of normal shops; that had to be bundled up and sold to the highest bidder in a cold and leaking cattle market that smelled of sheep shit and the sweat of frightened cows. In this place, though, Len saw himself king as he dropped bids with the raise of an eyebrow, bidding to lift prices in the hope of driving some of the others away. To clear space for the good stuff. *Sais dig,* they called him. Maggie knew what it meant but kept it to herself and while he did frustrate things for the locals from time to time, they all agreed that Len was worth the extra few pennies for the show he put on and the way that he cleared the lots that no one else wanted.

But this one was different. Len could feel it as they rounded the bends that led them home to Trwm Ddu. The place was set high on the hillside at the end of a steep drive. It might have been called picturesque had not the rhododendrons and nettles been left to run riot; had the little place not been surrounded by a clutter of outbuildings, all in various states of neglect. These might have added charm to such an isolated place deep in the Powys wilderness had it been tidy and the pathways neat. The image of healthy plump hens strutting in and out of tumble-down barns and rooting amongst daffodils and bluebells; of lazy cats sunning on weathered beams in the hazy afternoon might have been endearing, but the image was ruined by the butchered cars and greasy engine parts that littered the place. Of oil stains and tyre marks that spoiled the grassy verges and the constant stench of petrol where the odour of lavender might have otherwise carried on the breeze.

The largest of the outbuildings was the ancient haybarn that stood precariously on stilts like a raised-up Anderson shelter and blocked most of the morning sun from the kitchen window. It leaned ominously towards the deep gulley and the brook, its waters rising and falling according to the wash-off. That it leaned this way was, however, considerably preferable to having it lean the *other* way – towards the little house. Maggie would often stand at the sink as she cut and chopped and prepared dinner and gaze at the ugly old thing wondering what the view was like beyond.

But it was Len's barn; his sanctuary: the place he went to hide from the world. The place he could hang up the naughty calendars and think she hadn't noticed. Where he could sit, if he was so minded, and reflect on a few things. But mostly it was where he could fiddle and sort and dream of being king of the auction room.

He was dreaming this very dream as he pulled to the gate at the bottom of the drive and waited for his wife to open it. He didn't ever think to stop and let her back in once he had driven through. Was always too busy taking in the place and all that he owned, leaving Maggie to trudge up the hill and be surrounded by frantic hens and hungry cats. At the top of the drive, in the house, he could hear the dogs yelping at the sound of the van labouring up the hill and the first spots of rain began to fall from a darkening sky.

Come on love, won't take a sec, said Len as he creaked up the barn steps to open the trap-door. Maggie leaned against one of the wooden supports that held the whole thing up and caught her breath. As she did so she could feel the timber also breathe and shift in the strengthening wind, clicking and sighing under the load of countless second-Thursday trips. She noticed how the pile of chopped logs had depleted: another job she would have to do while the Lord of the Manor played with his toys.

I'll put the tea on first, love, she said, as she left her husband to move his own boxes. She had work to do.

By the time the chickens, cats and dogs had been fed, the stove lit, the kettle put on and dinner chopped and prepared, Len had lugged the boxes and sacks up the steps and was slumped in a fading wing-back amongst other boxes and sacks. He was fiddling with one of the old clocks when he heard her footsteps on the stairs.

What about this, then? he said as her head appeared in the hole in the floor. He was beaming stupidly and eager to show-off what he had bought. Maggie smiled and placed his mug on the floor. *Listen*.

After a little fumbling they both heard the whirring of tiny motion somewhere deep in the bowels of the clock. A sound they were both familiar with in the lonely hours of the night, awake and at the mercy of their thoughts. A sound that was a precursor to a more definitive one, one that nicked away another fraction of their lives. But this one was different. It wasn't the usual chime that the little clock put out but a softer, more melodious one.

It was a tune she remembered from some impossibly distant time when she was a girl. It was a song from a nursery rhyme. More ungraspable memories.

Lovely, dear, she said, then disappeared back down the steps, wanting to escape the sound, drown it out with her own and with it, maybe, her thoughts.

Within a few minutes Len could hear the familiar sound of Maggie below with the saw and chopper. He was comforted by the vibrations as teeth bit grain, the satisfying thump of split logs falling into the barrow, the smell of freshly wounded wood. He might have wondered, as he fumbled through a dusted parcel of notebooks labelled 'Bloomsbury', or something similar, containing hand-written notes from people he had never heard of – notes mostly to do with London written by people called Strachey and Keynes in handwriting he could hardly read or be bothered to decipher properly. He might have wondered if his wife had to make quite so much noise as she sawed and cut and he tried hard to read these notes and letters and see if they might be worth anything. But mostly he was comforted that she was near and that she was doing what she normally did.

He was disappointed with the parcel of notes and letters. Had seen a few greedy eyes on it at the auction house and paid a little more than he'd wanted to on the strength of that. But he was not impressed with the whining tone of the notes and this letter signed *V. Stephens* was hardly worth kindling the fire with. He dropped it onto the nearest pile of *Readers Digest* and *National Geographic* that leaned against the wooden wall, shifting with the subtle vibrations of the sawing below.

The sawing stopped, he heard the tools being dropped into their place behind the beams. The dunk of wood into the barrow and *dinner's in five – come down now, eh?*

I will, love. Be down in a tick. Just need to file this lot.

Anything else worth anything in there? Maggie said, only half-interested. She gazed at her own work, at the gashes in the timber, the fresh wood split and weeping, at the towers of stuff through the gap in the ceiling. At the piles of old television sets – the ancient heavy sort with the glass tube; at transistor radios. There was even an upright piano they had somehow hoisted up last summer. She had heard him try to play it two, three times before declaring it broken. Now it was a shelf for malformed porcelain dolls. At least five fruit machines, long since pillaged for spare change and now sad sentries to better times, stood slumped against the walls. Again she thought of a different time: a time of noise and cigarette smoke, of people and conversation.

Maggie marvelled at how the floor above her bowed in the middle; how it sagged and hung over the wood piles below like a full nappy. How box after box, bag after bag would go up those steps and never come back down.

Not sure yet. Still a couple to go, Len said, as he perched another parcel of loose papers and journals on a pile of magazines from a different century.

Got you a present though, he said, handing her down a box. *Don't say I don't treat you.*

The faint flicker of hope in Maggie's heart that this might

be something real – something she could latch on to for a better tomorrow – was extinguished when she saw what was in the box: seven grey bottles of industrial toilet cleaner; dozens of scourers; a pack (opened) of rubber gloves and three sink plungers. She smiled and headed towards the house, leaving the gift on the woodpile. As she did so Maggie felt the whole structure shift with the wind that was growing outside. She shivered, pulled her cardigan close and went inside. Rain pattered on the tin roof.

At dinner it was Len who did most of the talking as usual and Maggie who did most of the agreeing, though tonight she was a little more distant than usual. Her eyes wandered from time to time to Len's face and over his shoulder. Out of the window and across the miles of space and darkness to the distant orange pricks of street lights of the tiny town far away in the night.

You ok, love? he said. *I've been banging on for ages about how we could be on to something with these clocks and you've not said a word.* Maggie for an instant stared at her husband like she would stare at a stranger. Or a dead man. Not a trace of recognition in her eyes. Then was snapped back rudely, shocked at how she'd let herself slide again.

Sorry, love, she said, *I was looking at those clouds. It'll rain hard soon and we've not enough wood for the morning.*

Be enough for tonight, won't it? Len said, wiping bean juice from his chin.

Maggie was watching another shiny bean make its way steadily along its own juice down his chest. She noticed as it met the ketchup stain and hung for a moment before dropping into his lap. He never noticed, just batted absentmindedly at the dog which had jumped into his crotch to retrieve it. *Not if we need to make one up in the morning. I'll go and get some more.*

69

With that she was gone into the night. Len watched as the wind, that had indeed picked up, whipped the door from her hands and clawed at her clothes. Rain tapped at the kitchen windows and Len had an odd compulsion to go and help his wife bring in the firewood.

He took a deep swig of his beer, leaned back in the chair which creaked under his weight and wiped his mouth with the back of his hand. *Plenty of time*, he belched, to no one.

In the gloom lit only by the single bulb that hung on its own cord from the weathered wooden struts of the barn, Maggie busied herself with loading sawn chunks of timber onto the barrow and cursing her husband as she went about it. Outside the wind played with loose bits of cladding and worried the tin roof sheets. The more she thought and the more she cursed, the more she put into sawing. Sawing at timber. Moving from one corner to the other. Cursing up a storm and calling on the winds to blow and the rains to fall. Lost again in her thoughts as the saw bit clawed and cut until there was little left to do and she stood, cold with sweat and rain and ignoring the blisters that wept painfully into her palms.

The mausoleum above shifted and moaned like an old arthritic as she paused, hands on her knees, and breathed deep of the damp air. Only then did she notice Len's figure framed in the doorway, his shadow reaching across to where she stood so that the stretched neck lay across the teeth of the saw in her hand, the shadow of the axe buried deep in the small of his shadow back.

For certain she knew that he had been standing there all this time; had been watching her, hearing her. Had seen what she was really up to and the damage that she had done; what she had been doing stealthily over time.

He stepped forward into the barn, saw teeth biting into

shadow neck and Maggie didn't move. The only sounds the laboured breathing of the tired barn, the crunch of footsteps on sawdust and somewhere impossibly distant:

Turn again Dick Whittington
Right Lord Mayor of London Town

Sweet bells. The *taptap* of heavy rain on the tin roof high above. The settling sigh, the weight of the years; the pressures of time; the weathering wearing of life. The slow consistent creaking of the pillars that had held her upright all these years.

But his words weren't murderous and his voice had that same daft obtuseness; his face the same hopeful expression as always. *You alright, love?* he said, *you look a mess.*

Fine. All done, Maggie said.

Well, that thing's just started on the telly. I came to give you a hand.

She placed the saw against the beam in the corner, knowing it was the last time she'd ever do so and to herself, repeated slowly:

Done now.

Then watched her husband climb the steps.

I'm just going to get that clock, Len said, *don't like to leave it out here in this, just in case. You know.*

Almost calling him back, almost changing her mind, before he disappeared through the trapdoor hole, she turned with the barrow of firewood towards the house.

The structure complained violently as Len padded across the floor. New groans mixed with old. A wail of tortured cats in the mix with the wind and the rain. Splitting and wrenching. A tearing sound, hardly perceptible but there, definitely there. And new sounds.

***

Maggie padded across the yard to the little house. It wasn't until she was back in the warmth of the kitchen, her wellingtons off and cardigan draped across the back of the sofa; not until she had dropped herself stiffly down and closed her eyes to the thought of what she had done that she heard it for real.

Above the wind that chased around outside and above the rain that hammered now on the roofs and windows. Above even the noise of the television that crowed to itself in the corner. Above the nervous whining of the dogs around her ankles. It was a new sound. A whole new world of sound that frightened her beyond the thought of what it represented. A massive sound; the sound a tree makes when it falls in a wood. A tempestuous ocean of complaint, the shifting of an unshiftable weight.

In her mind she saw it all. With the eye that is permanently awake she saw the lean that she had encouraged with her sawing; the lean that he had become used to steepen. Saw it list like a doomed ship in a fatal storm, corrupted supports inadequate for the new balance of weight and the wind pushing, urging. Saw it topple like a felled elephant, impossibly slow. Saw it fold in on itself, crumple and slide heavily and violently to rest in silent debris at the bottom of the gulley far below as the weight of it all crushed and destroyed itself. Saw even the stream make icy paths through the rubble of wood and stuff.

She saw it and heard it all as she sat there with her eyes closed in the warmth of the fire. Except his scream. She wouldn't hear that. Nor would she see in her mind her latest husband lying somewhere in the dark crushed by the weight of his own fruitless dreams.

Slowly Maggie stood and turned off the television. The new

noises seemed to have abated. The wind, having done its worst, had retreated and the rain had stopped altogether. It was a wall of silence she had not known in this house before and now that she had it, it frightened her in a way that she hadn't expected.

From outside a silver finger of moonlight picked its way across the darkness and over the little house. She stepped into the darkness, now chill in the sudden still and pulled her cardigan tighter around her, closing the dogs inside. Not a single sound, party over. Noise like a hole in the night and before her a gaping hole in the yard where the barn had once stood. Now only a dozen stumps, thick as an elephant's leg, stood in its place, pointing skywards like the drowning masts of some great ship. Half-sawn, half-wrenched.

From far below where the stream ran downhill to meet the river, nothing, save for the occasional flap of yellowed page, delicate as a moth's wings. From time to time settling weight filling gaps.

My Len, my love, she cried as she leaned over the edge of the drop. *I didn't mean for this. Not like this, Len. You weren't meant to be in there, I don't think. I don't know. Len?*

Nothing. Only the sound of the back door banging on its hinges and the dogs scampering out of the house and into the yard. Their frenzied barks brought Maggie back to herself and she turned towards the house and her new life.

***

By the time she had reached the kitchen she was smiling again, ruffling the coats of the dogs who were over their distress and happy to see her. She didn't bother to turn the television back on, there were jobs to do: to call 999 for a start, but first to sit back and take in the silence that had never been possible before. She sat and listened to the new sounds of the old house.

The house that was now all her own. Sounds she had never noticed before, like the way that the old timbers creaked and settled, sounding sometimes like someone creeping about in the rooms upstairs. The way that the remaining breeze outside caught in the chimney flue and played tunes in the wood burner like the sounds of a dying man. Timeless sounds that were brand new to her and that she relished as she breathed in her new freedom.

All except one.

A new sound that was very out of place in her house on this night. A sound as though from another world that drifted from the darkness of the rooms above her like a knell from some other world.

Maggie stood at the foot of the stairs, frozen in the ice of her terror and listened to the gentle tones of the Whittington chimes cascade down from the darkness.

Welcome to Momentum 2023

Emily Vanderploeg

Seren is poised at the entrance, guitar case swinging heavily from her hand, deciding where to sit. Hay bales have been positioned in a concentric circle within the yurt. From above, it would resemble the shape of an archer's target. The day is mild; it is early October, but the woodstove is working furiously, its chimney pipe pumping grey-white smoke out into the misty green landscape. Upon its hearth sits a tin jug filled with artfully arranged wildflowers. The sun casts a wan light upon the backs of half of the group, not quite reaching the faces of the others, instead resting upon the hands in their laps, which hold tin mugs of tisanes and filter coffee from a samovar. Some are wearing Gore-Tex or cashmere fingerless gloves.

We are comfortable with being uncomfortable. We came here to be challenged. Many of us have paid for the privilege to be challenged this week. We are comfortable with silence. Let's sit with that. How do you feel as we come to the end of our time here?

In the e-mail exchange, when Seren had asked what the theme of the event was, Ursula had replied that they were there 'to learn how to be the architects of a sustainable world.' Seren worried she didn't know how to be an architect of a sustainable world – she didn't want to upset anyone; it was a commission, after all, and a performance. She wanted to sing to the choir,

75

as it were. Ursula replied that they wanted to be disrupted and urged Seren not to censor herself and to please send her invoice by Saturday. A vegan lunch would be provided at the conclusion of the event.

Ursula appears at the entrance and greets Seren with a brisk, smiling hello, telling her to take a seat wherever. She is much younger and prettier than Seren expected: like the sort of person who skis regularly. After walking quietly around a quarter of the circle and sitting on an empty bale in the outer ring, Seren notices that Ursula has sat in the inner circle, and she is looking expectantly at the man who has just spoken. Seren observes the assembled group with an open face, curious yet worried she will be asked to participate. The group is sitting in silence, which she understands they have become accustomed to this week. They have learned to be comfortable with being uncomfortable; to sit with their thoughts, and to think about what brought them here. They have reflected and are ready to share their reflections. Seren wonders if she will like the vegan lunch, and notices spiderwebs, still heavy with dew, hanging above their heads on the plastic windows of the yurt.

When the silence has been sat in, Terrence, a man with wire-framed glasses and shaggy grey hair in his late fifties, begins. He rises to stand in the centre of the target, smooths out his chinos, and speaks slowly, with an ambiguously foreign accent, maybe German or Australian, inviting the attendees to notice five arrows he has placed on the floor, written on chart paper.

These openings in the circle represent how you entered this process and how you are leaving today.

He rotates his body to point at each one in turn:

ACTION > FEELING > QUESTION > CONNECTION > WILD CARD

Terrence then demonstrates, skipping swiftly between the hay bales and taking a quick circuit of the circle before pausing at ACTION and treading over it to return to the centre.

I arrived here on Monday believing that our presence was the first step in taking action. But I leave here... [he turns slowly on his heel] *...relishing the connections I've made, and hoping that these new relationships – both professional and personal – continue to open something within me when I reflect upon our roles in combatting the climate crisis – together.*

Terrence exits the circle over CONNECTION and re-enters again through WILD CARD to take his seat. He opens his hands on his knees in a silent invitation for others to share as he has done.

Bits of straw poke through Seren's long cardigan, pressing into her backside. She arches her back, even though she hasn't been sitting long. No one else seems uncomfortable. Seren notices that everyone's skin in the yurt has a dewy, fresh pallor. All of the men are tall.

A few people stand up and take their places at different entrances to the circle. It soon becomes a fluid stream of people,

IN → *I came here with a lot of questions about my role, as someone who works to promote the oil and gas industry –* and OUT *– I'm leaving feeling frustrated. I wanted to feel more uncomfortable; more challenged on my role.* →

→ *I arrived with curiosity as to how this particular group would work together to take action and I leave here feeling hopeful about the future of our environment, and like I can be part of the action for change.* →

→ *As a scientist, I naturally arrived here with questions, even rather dubious ones, as to the intentions of certain people here… and I leave here feeling… surprised that there has been a genuine openness to change. But… I think some of my first questions remain…*→

→ *I arrived really with the whole Wild Card thing, you know, I wasn't sure what to expect and then I met Marcus.* [a chorus of laughter] *And now, I leave here with so many connections – you know who you are! – and I'm excited for us to work with each other on bold, forward-thinking initiatives once we leave this place.* →

Seren notices that many people refer to "this place", but few of them seem to mention or notice that this place is in Wales. She wonders if her song choice – a bilingual folk ballad that she wrote about the resurgence of the red kite – might be ill-judged. Should she just sing in English? In her head, Seren runs through other songs she could play, considering this and that, as people pop up from their hay bales and move like a swirling sort of organism in and out of the sharing circle. Just when she thinks it's nearing its end, two young women enter the circle together. They are different from the rest of the group – one is black (the only non-white person in the yurt) and has her septum pierced, the other has long dreadlocks and her ribcage exposed by her crop top. They are dressed in a combination of the following: a bucket hat, pink coveralls, Doc Marten boots, Crocs, a multi-coloured crocheted vest, an oversized lime-green T-shirt, wide-leg ragged-edged jeans, a black and white Bedouin scarf.

→ *Right, so, basically yeah, we arrived here feeling like we did not want to be here. Like... Ursula asked us, and we were honestly like, seriously resistant.*

Yeah, like, we just felt like, why should we be here to help you people see the other side, you feel me? And honestly, we arrived here feeling angry.

Yeah. For real.

And I think we leave here, still with a lot of anger, and a lot of feelings, a lot of them not good. Like... we have met and talked to people here and been surprised, like that's fair, for real. Like I didn't want to like any of you, you get me? [uncomfortable laughter] *But, I still feel frustrated. Like I feel like the magnitude of change that needs to happen has not been fully acknowledged and like you're all just going to leave here today feeling really good about yourselves and like, nothing real is gonna change. Do you wanna add anything, babe?*

No, like, that's basically it. I guess I'm leaving with a question, and that is – who here is accountable? →

Seren sits up straighter. The energy of the yurt has shifted and she realises that she is enjoying sitting within discomfort. She decides to sing her original song after all.

The people waiting to enter the circle now step in with more purpose and intensity.

→ *I arrived here ready to take action and wanting to learn how and I leave here feeling... full of shame.* →

→ *At the beginning of this week I had so many questions about the world and now…* [holds hands gently to abdomen, closes eyes and sways slowly] *I leave feeling my importance as a mother-to-be* [mild gasps of surprise] *and my connection to the earth… and the life I am growing inside of me and the society we are creating…*→

→ *When I arrived here I had a lot of questions about my place in the world and then I had so many deep, deep conversations, late at night by the fire – Marcus! – and now, golly gosh, I'm leaving here with so many feelings, which I think are actually revelations, like… about my father, who I think never really loved me…*→

Seren scans the faces of those in the yurt, and sees that many eyes are closed, tears rolling down cheeks, or bowed deeply, as if in prayer. She glances over her shoulder at the two angry young activists, and sees that one is rolling a cigarette and the other's narrowed eyes are fixed on the man whose father didn't love him, as he exits the circle through FEELING. Seren decides to sing her song entirely in Welsh.

The queue of people moving through the circle has finally slowed, and Terrence returns to the centre. He stands expectantly, like a teacher waiting for the students at assembly to quiet, even though the only sounds are of the fire in the stove crackling, birds twittering, and the distant sound of dishes and pans in preparation for the vegan lunch.

Wow. What a testament to the week we've shared together. Thank you all for opening yourselves to each other – this is what the Momentum Conference is all about. It's a shame that we're missing so many people today, who had to leave early to head back to work and to beat the traffic into central London, but they have left with us their spirit this week. To close out our session, I'd now like to welcome musician, eco-poet, artist of this land we have been so privileged to occupy this week – Sa-ren Davies.

Seren rises, lifting her guitar by the neck, and enters the centre of the circle, where Ursula places a microphone and a wooden stool. As Seren places her notes on the stool beside her, a handful of people, including the two activists, slip out of the yurt, one after the other, tin cups in hand. She clears her throat, and begins to tell the remaining group about the near extinction of the red kite, and how one bird in Wales saved the entire species – a beacon of hope to us all.

This song is called 'Mae'r barcud coch yn ffenics'.

Seren plucks the strings of her guitar at a slow tempo and as she begins to strum, she closes her eyes as her folk contralto fills the yurt with birds of prey and descriptions of the fields and forest beyond, where she has walked and played and watched her *tadcu* farm and where she has smoked joints and drunk cheap cider and kissed boys in concrete bus stops. She imagines a red kite soaring high above the yurt as her voice carries in melody the language of her *mamgu*, of school, of work, sometimes, and of her own home.

As she ends with a soft, high note, turning to face everyone in the yurt with her guitar as she strums the final chords, most of the people have either bowed their heads again, or their gazes are fixed on some middle distance, perhaps with thoughts of their imminent lunch. They seem to startle themselves with their applause, raising their heads to smile at Seren as she blushes, nodding her thanks.

Diolch yn fawr, it sounds like you've had an absolutely incredible week here, diolch again for inviting me and I hope you enjoyed.

Seren returns to her hay bale, placing her guitar in its case, and closes the latches. An older woman nearby leans across the aisle to tell her, *Da iawn!*

Ursula returns to the circle and begins an award-show chorus of thanks.

Thanks so much, Seren. That was brilliant, and a really great reminder of why we chose to come to this place this year. [she claps, others follow] *And of course, I need to thank the phenomenal human that is Marcus for marshalling us through this week and helping us to find our centres.* [hearty applause]

Marcus is sitting on the outer ring of the circle, knees wide apart, feet together, his upturned wrists balancing on his knees. He is wearing a khaki boiler suit, but Seren doesn't remember him putting it on, only that he wasn't wearing it earlier, before she realised that he was the ubiquitous Marcus. He closes his eyes and holds his hands up to Ursula in a gesture of prayer. The applause stills and Ursula goes on:

Thank you to Terrence for being our leader and guide through this process. You know, I arrived here five days ago in work mode. Like, I really didn't want to mess up this opportunity that Terrence had given me after we met – so randomly, when I found his phone at Knightsbridge station! – the Universe really made this connection happen. And, you know, climate is something I am so passionate about, as well as event planning and women in corporate leadership and I… well, fuck it, when I got here on Monday I came on my period, and I thought – can I really do this? And then I've spent the week watching everyone being so vulnerable and I feel that I've learned to be vulnerable, too, and I just think that is so brave because being vulnerable is FUCKING hard. [rousing applause] *Organising Momentum has been an honour and I just want to thank all of you for this life-changing week – THANK YOU.*

Terrence rises to conclude the session.

And finally, before we go to our lunches, and then away from this place where we have been so changed, let us think our fearless organiser, Ursula. Words cannot express our thanks, so I'll ask everyone to close our eyes now and take a moment to think about our gratitude for Ursula.

Fat tears roll down Ursula's thin, porcelain cheeks. The enormous fur bobble on her hat quivers as she takes in everyone's silent, reverential gratitude to her. Seren bows her head because she desperately wants to laugh, but does not close her eyes. She furtively watches the group's still, furrowed brows as Ursula cries silently, sniffing and wiping her nose on the back of her gloved hand.

When everyone slowly opens their eyes and raises their heads at Terrence's behest, they rise, stretch, and move towards the sun-dappled outdoor canteen, where a fire blazes in an open stone pit, and picnic tables are arranged with expensive Welsh wool blankets on the benches and a view of the countryside beyond. Seren queues for an aubergine, butternut squash, and sorrel and walnut pesto bap with potato wedges and microgreens, and pours herself a glass of lavender and elderflower presse. She sits at a large table, but no one joins her. They are all saying goodbyes, queueing for the outdoor toilet, and getting extra baps for their journeys over the Severn bridge back to England. Seren concedes, the vegan lunch is delicious.

After returning her dishes to the outdoor kitchen wash bins, Seren scans the group to find Ursula, approaching her by the open fire to thank her for the opportunity.

No, thank you! It was such a brilliant end to the week. I guess you'll have gathered that we've had quite a special time here. I absolutely loved that you sang in Welsh – thanks for leaning into the discomfort!

Right, yeah. Dim problem.

What? Oh, haha! Was that Welsh? I love that. And you've emailed your invoice to me, yeah?

Yep, sent last night. Anyways, I'm off. You don't know when the bus passes by here, do you?

Ah, no, sorry. Maybe ask one of the permanent staff? Thanks again.

Ursula turns back to her lunch and Terrence and Marcus, who are deep in conversation.

With her guitar case swinging heavily, Seren walks slowly up the long, narrow drive that she notes was not long ago a farmer's lane. Whose farm was this? Is this Cefn-gorwydd? Tadcu would know. As she reaches the car park, she's surprised to see Gethin, hoisting two bin bags into a skip.

Hiya Geth! Alright?

Seren, mun, what you doing here?

Singing for the esteemed guests, weren't I?

Ah, fair play. Heading home now, is it?

If the bus ever comes.

Ah look, I'm going in 10 if you fancy a lift. That's my car there.

Shiny black Range Rover or rusty red Ford Fiesta?

Cheeky. [he laughs]

Anyways, cheers Geth, that's brill. I'll just hang out here 'til you're done.

Tidy. Won't be long now.

Gethin hurries back to the conference centre and Seren sits on a large oak stump, leaning her guitar case against the remaining hedgerow. A robin and two sparrows flit in and out of the holly and blackthorn, and Seren angles her face up towards the bright, cloudless sky, just in time to glimpse a pair of red kites soaring and then disappearing beyond the treeline.

Save the Maiden

Bethan L. Charles

Six fingers poked out of the mud where the barley once grew. Rhiannon slotted a basket into the curve of her waist, hitched up her tunic, and squelched through the field. She plucked a finger from the earth. Its silver band glistened in the midsummer sun, but the metal refused to slide over the bloodied knuckle. She'd have to use a knife later. Dropping the mess of flesh and bone into her basket, she continued sifting through the churned ground, and collected coins, mangled bait hooks, and rings (with or without fingers attached) until she stumbled on a feathered body entangled in barley florets. Poor thing. She tilted her head to the clear sky and sang her favourite blessing.

'Rhiannon!' Her father's bellow pierced her melody.

He stood in front of their stone cottage, tapping a foot on the slate path, his new leather boots catching the light. She glanced at her own sandalled feet, caked in mud, then at her basket – one silver and two bronze rings, five bait hooks for smelting, and an assortment of coins. It might be enough to buy her leather boots this time.

'What'd we get, my girl?' her father asked as she shuffled towards him.

She relinquished her basket and, as he counted the spoils from the flood, she checked Dyfri's shack behind their cottage. It stood untouched. Ice quenched the hope she'd allowed to blossom in her chest.

Sin. It was a sin to wish death on a man, her father's loyal ploughman, no less. And yet…

'These rings aren't enough to cover the lost harvest,' her father said. 'The beast'll pay for these floods, but remember, don't you dare wander near the afanc's pool, my girl.'

'Yes, Father.'

He brandished a severed finger before tossing it back into the basket. 'If that demon does this to our brave fishermen and hunters, no telling what it'd do to a fair maiden.' He brushed her chin with his calloused hand. 'And I got the fairest in the whole valley.'

Maiden. Rhiannon's gaze flicked to Dyfri's shack.

***

Summer dissolved into an empty harvest. The village plundered last year's grain stores and unease settled over the valley, hanging heavy like the clouds cloaking the sun.

'A hunting party leaves tomorrow,' Rhiannon's father announced one breakfast.

Again? Hardly any returned.

'Who'll till the fields?' Rhiannon asked.

'Have faith. They'll beat the beast, but I can ask our Dyfri to stay, if that settles you. He's a good lad.'

Rhiannon toyed with her stale bread. She'd almost confessed to the unspeakable many times, but what good would come of it? They owed Dyfri. After the afanc's first flood injured her father, Rhiannon's futile efforts in draining their fields by hand had almost broken her body. It was then that Dyfri arrived with his stallion and plough. Their saviour. Without him, they'd have lost their farm. So, of course, she was proud of winning his attention at first. She had encouraged it.

She'd blushed when he first tucked her stray hair behind her ear. Then, last Harvest, she had been the one to linger, waiting for privacy, agreeing to that stroll along the river. Ultimately, their sin was her fault.

As she picked at the dirt caked under her fingernails, her father chuckled, seeming to misplace her nerves for coyness, and his gaze flicked over the curves hidden under her woollen mantle.

'I think it's time we invite Dyfri for dinner,' he said.

Despite the roaring hearth, Rhiannon shivered.

The following dawn, she scooped rings, fingers, and shattered pitchforks into her basket.

***

The frost thawed. Daffodils sprouted and green washed over the valley. The stream swelled only with meltwater, but dread blossomed in the village. The fishing season approached, and people were terrified the monster's flood would strike again.

'I'm visiting Betws-y-Coed,' Rhiannon's father said, packing his cart. 'Rumour is other villages have defeated their monsters. We're going to learn how. End this demon's reign of terror. Dyfri will look after you. Be good.'

'Yes, Father.'

Horse hooves thudded beside Rhiannon, and Dyfri towered above, lifting a hand in farewell. The brass thumb band he'd salvaged from the last flood glinted in the dawn light. After her father disappeared around the valley, Dyfri stared down, baring his unusually straight teeth in a smile that lit his dark eyes. Her father would've thought it charming, but she knew the promise lurking within. She'd avoided the first dinners with Dyfri, blaming her monthly curse, but once her father became wise of her natural rhythm, he'd adjusted his invites. So, for weeks, she'd endured Dyfri's earthen stench in her home and shrunk against the approval growing in her father's gaze.

'What luck is this?' Dyfri said, climbing down from the horse. The sound of his deep, lilting voice raised the hairs on the back of her neck. 'The entire cottage just for us. As if it were ours already.' He stepped closer.

She jumped back. 'D-Dandelions.' She could escape under the pretence of foraging ingredients for soup.

'What?'

'For dinner,' she said.

'Why eat weeds when we have rabbits?'

'We'll run out if we continue catching so many.'

'It's impossible to run out of rabbits.' He edged closer. There was no escape, unless…

'I am not strong enough to chase down rabbits. I need you.'

Dyfri toyed with Rhiannon's stray hair. 'You do.'

When he galloped towards the rabbit warrens, Rhiannon seized her chance. She grabbed her basket and hurried into the woods leading up the mountain, darting around gnarled oaks, jumping over brooks, and hopping between moss-covered boulders.

Run, run, run. Higher, higher.

She climbed beyond the steps that defeated horses. Her urgency clouded her senses until she almost stumbled into a lake. No. A pool.

The afanc's pool.

Bones littered the stony shore. Fishing boats stuck out of trees that towered above the silken water, black as night despite the bright sky. She had to flee this evil place, the demon's lair, but fear glued her feet.

Then the surface rippled. A jagged hide pierced the water. Rhiannon wanted to scream, but she watched as if detached from her body – like those nights in the shack. The beast heaved itself out of the shallows and rose to half an oak's height. The fur lining its underbelly seemed to devour light, but its scales glittered like moss after rain. Its long snout hinged open, revealing three rows of serrated teeth, before its growl rumbled through the earth and the smell of rotten flesh filled the air.

Trembling, Rhiannon lifted her gaze away from the monster and towards the birds soaring above. She sang to soothe her impending doom.

Up to the heavens, past the sun, the stars,
Free from the chains of Earth's sins and scars.

The beast stopped growling.

Free of those who clip your wings,
Free of the bars prison brings.

A melodic rumble shook the ground. Had she imagined it, or was the demon *mimicking* her song? Rhiannon met the afanc's gaze. The black irises slicing through its green eyes widened. It tapped the stones with its foot-long claws, as if impatient for her to continue. This was her chance. If singing distracted the monster, she might have time to run.

Joining those of centuries past,
Sharing peace at long last.

Water sprayed Rhiannon's face as the afanc thrashed its broad tail in…. pleasure? Was this a dream? A vision sent by God to save her from the pain of the demon shredding her body? Except the icy water felt so real.

When the beast calmed, it dug its claws into the ground and closed its eyes. Rhiannon seized her chance to run. She dropped her basket and fled into the woods. But the afanc's growl shook her bones, and she stopped as its song rumbled through her mind, its lyrics resonating like ethereal echoes.

Safe in a home of water and weed,

Fish to grow, fish to feed.

Rhiannon faced the monster.

Balanced a century, a life ideal.

Then demons arrive, poised to steal.

The muscles in the afanc's arms tensed.

Defend the home, defend the fish,

Fail, and summon a final wish.

The creature tilted its snout to the fishing boats anchored in the surrounding trees. Rhiannon wanted to feel horrified, disgusted, frightened.

Instead, she asked, 'How?'

The corners of the afanc's mouth creased into what might have been a smile.

***

Three days later, the rabbits on the farm disappeared.

Dyfri did not forage. After all, it was a woman's work, though for Rhiannon it was the perfect excuse to escape. She had not intended to return to the afanc's pool, but when she slipped out the forest, the creature was waiting, as if it knew her return was inevitable.

***

Rhiannon visited the afanc's pool the next day, and the next, and the next. The creature sang the secrets of the valley and from them Rhiannon learnt how to pick nettles to avoid being stung, how to harvest dandelions without killing the plant, how to prune a berry bush to protect the fruit from rot. The lessons kept her away from Dyfri all day. But not all night. Obviously, she never confessed her lack of innocence to the creature, although, on the first visit after breaking free of Dyfri's clutches, its song was gentler, as though it wanted to comfort her in a way an embrace from its granite-hard claws could not.

Soon, she craved the creature's company.

During her seventh visit, she rested on the shoreline beside the dozing afanc. Its chest rippled, revealing a mesmerising iridescence folded within its black fur. How could this beautiful creature be the monster her father warned her of?

With a deep breath, she gathered the courage to ask, 'Why do you destroy our harvest and kill our fishermen?'

The afanc huffed, growling its song without raising its head.

Give and take, take and give, nothing to forgive,
But steal and chop and burn, then expect a fair return.

The Lord spoke ill of revenge, but who was Rhiannon to judge? How often had she wished for the afanc's floods to claim Dyfri and crack his skull against boulders? In her darkest dreams, she'd watched as the creature's claws shredded his hands. His hands…

She stroked the bruises encircling her wrists.

***

Ten days after meeting the afanc, Dyfri blocked her path into the woods.

'We have plenty of weeds,' he said. 'Don't leave me lonely again.'

When she tried to escape, he wrapped his arm around her

shoulder. She twisted in his grip, glimpsing the afanc's mountain rising into the heavens before Dyfri led her to Hell. Afterwards, as he slept, she escaped to the pool and, despite pouring her energy into sucking in her tears, she lost control and let her dam burst. The creature stayed silent until her eyes ran dry. Shame consumed her. She wanted nothing more than to run. Find solitude. Only then might she find peace from her turbulent mind.

She sprinted into the woods.

But the afanc hooked a claw into the hem of her tunic and started rumbling tunes with lyrics that would've made even her father's cheeks turn holly berry red. Only when the creature finished did Rhiannon realise their shared laughter had calmed her thoughts.

'So that's how you spend the years,' she said, wiping her nose with her stained shawl. 'Making up lewd songs.'

The afanc swept its claw over the mountains. *Not my songs.*

'There are more like you?'

The creature hung its head.

***

A month after meeting the afanc, Rhiannon's father returned. He marched into the barley field as she walked out of the woods.

'Where've you been?' her father asked.

'Foraging.'

'Ha! No more weed soup.' He embraced her. 'We know how to defeat the monster.'

She whimpered.

'Don't be afraid. This time, we have the right weapons. Ah,

93

my boy, we need you.' He smiled as Dyfri appeared, then stroked Rhiannon's cheek. 'Stay home. This is not for innocent eyes.'

The afanc's first flood had almost killed her father. He wouldn't survive a hunt, and without him, she'd be at Dyfri's mercy. She shivered at the memories of fingers sticking out of the barley field. She had to save her father from the afanc's vengeance. But the afanc was right to be angry. Rhiannon now knew of the grief fuelling its rage. Fear washed over her as she realised the neighbouring villages had caused that grief, and her father had been away meeting the village leaders, learning how to murder the creature.

No. She would not lose her father or her friend.

After the men left, she raced into the woods, past the oaks, brooks, and boulders to the pool where the afanc dozed under the afternoon sun.

Back so soon? the afanc rumbled in her mind.

'Leave,' she said.

Its lizard eyes opened.

'The villagers are hunting again.'

The afanc glanced at the fishing boats wedged in the trees and shrugged its mighty shoulders.

'Please. My father's leading them.'

The creature huffed.

'He doesn't deserve to be hurt.'

The ridges over the afanc's eyes inverted.

'If he's injured. If he… If he dies, I lose everything.'

Defend the home, defend the fish.

'I'm defending *my* home.'

Defending Hell?

Silence hung between them.

'Sing to them,' she said. 'Like you sing to me. Tell them they're ruining your home.'

No.

'Why?'

The afanc tapped a claw against its temple. *They do not listen, so they cannot hear.*

'Then I'll tell them.'

The afanc sighed. The weight of the truth in its gaze made Rhiannon slump onto the pebbles. They were two creatures with silent songs. She couldn't save her father or her friend.

A roar broke their silence. Men sprang from the trees, led by Rhiannon's father, pitchfork raised.

'My girl, don't move. I'll save you,' he said, racing forwards.

The afanc snarled as it rose to its hind legs and lifted its claws, casting the men in shadow.

Rhiannon screamed.

The afanc hesitated, giving her father time to strike, but he staggered when his pitchfork bent against the creature's scales. The afanc scooped him into a tree and Rhiannon's father bellowed for her. She ran for him, but someone hurled her over their shoulder; their brass thumb ring dug into her arm.

'I've got you,' Dyfri said.

She bit his hand, and a metallic tang stung her tongue.

'Damn, girl.' Dyfri dropped Rhiannon. 'I'm saving you, you foolish—'

Rhiannon wrapped her arms around Dyfri's ankles and pushed against a rock. He tumbled into the pool behind him as she scrambled to her feet.

'*You* will not hurt my friend.'

Fury carved Dyfri's face when he rose from the water. He waded forwards with his hands clenched and Rhiannon shielded her head, prepared for his fist, but the blow never came; instead, Dyfri shrieked. The afanc had trapped him beneath its claws. Its roar shook the mountain.

'Now!' Dyfri shouted.

A giant of a man clad in blacksmith leathers shackled the afanc's wrists in irons thicker than an ox's neck. The creature thrashed and released Dyfri, who raced to Rhiannon, and trapped her against his chest as the blacksmith's iron spear caught the afanc's underbelly. It squealed, then it stilled, gazing at Rhiannon squirming in Dyfri's arms.

Defend the home, defend the fish,
Fail, and summon a final wish.

An ethereal melody rippled over the pool. Waves transformed to rapids. The men screamed as the water churned and swelled, swallowing their feet, legs, waists, heads.

When the blacksmith slipped under the surface, the afanc leapt forwards, claws slicing. A wall of water then slammed into Rhiannon and Dyfri, tearing them apart and sweeping her down the mountainside. Helplessly, she fought the torrent, certain a rock would crack her skull, and she'd be lost to eternal darkness.

But she evaded every boulder as the water carried her in its soft embrace.

***

The next day, eleven fingers stuck out of the barley field. Rhiannon and her father knelt in the mud, salvaging their remaining crops.

'That demon can't hurt you anymore,' her father had said once he'd returned from the healer. He hadn't spoken since.

Rhiannon worked in silence, trawling through the ruined earth, pausing only when she discovered a brass thumb ring glinting in the spring light.

Bricks and Sticks

Rachel Powell

The man from Steadman and Sons is back to put up the 'For Sale' sign. He carries it into the garden, slung over his left shoulder like he's one of Snow White's friends taking a pickaxe down to the mine, and in his right hand he holds a lump hammer. He chooses a spot on Hal's perfectly green, perfectly manicured lawn – close enough to the front of the garden so it's clearly visible to pedestrians, but far enough back to draw the eye towards the quaint little cottage and its backdrop of evergreen trees – then he sets to work, piercing the garden with the blunted spike at the bottom of the sign and pounding it into the ground. The dull thunk of rubber hitting wood makes me feel sick.

'Vultures,' I whisper under my breath. There's a mug of tea in my hands, and I'm squeezing it so hard, it's a miracle it doesn't break.

'It's okay, Jen,' Hal says quietly. 'It's just a house. Just bricks and sticks, that's all.'

It doesn't feel okay.

Outside, the man (who probably isn't Steadman *or* one of his sons) thwacks the sign one last time, then gives it a wobble with his foot, making sure it's in deep enough. Satisfied, he strides back across the garden, closing the gate behind him as he leaves. Over the top of the wall I watch him open the back of his bright yellow van, throw in the lump hammer, and close it again. He wipes his hands on his trousers, then walks round to the driver's side and climbs in. He doesn't even glance towards the house. They've probably warned him not to, after last time.

I watch until the van disappears around the corner, and then I place my mug down and turn away from the window, sagging back against the counter as I look around the kitchen. Packing is already well underway, so it's a bit of a mess. Open-topped boxes fill almost every available surface, each stuffed to the brim with old saucepans and cutlery and bubble-wrapped glasses. The freezer's already been emptied of every last ice-burned chicken breast, every solitary frozen pea, but there's still the medicine cupboard to look through, and the glass-fronted cabinets up on the wall to sort out: shelves and shelves of mismatched cups and saucers from old, stained tea sets, cracked teapots, chipped gravy boats and commercial eggcups, acquired at Easter with an accompanying chocolate egg and never used. There are sheaves of paperwork shoved behind the kettle and the bread bin and the microwave – letters and bills and newspapers and instruction manuals. Hal has always been a little bit of a hoarder, though he's gotten worse since Mum died. I did try to organise things a bit, but he wasn't having any of it.

'You just never know when you might need something, see, Jen,' he says now as I get back to work, emptying the remains of my tea down the sink and picking up a couple of circulars advertising new bathrooms from behind the toaster. 'Waste not, want not.'

I roll my eyes.

'You won't ever need these,' I tell him, throwing the circulars into the bin. He doesn't answer.

Hal has lived in this house for as long as I've known him.

As I potter around the kitchen, I picture him, clear as anything, holding open the front door for us on the day Mum and I moved in, a huge smile on his face.

'You were so big and round and raucous,' I tell him as I whizz a cloth over the kitchen table, mopping up ring marks, 'like a sandy-haired Father Christmas.'

'Are you saying I was fat?!'

'I'm saying you were... jolly.'

'Jolly I can live with,' he says, and I can hear the smile in his voice.

I remember covering my face with my hands and hiding behind Mum, but Hal had kneeled down on the floor and looked me right in the eyes.

'I want you to be happy here,' he'd said. 'What would make you happiest?'

'I want to go back to my old house,' I'd said, close to tears. He'd glanced at Mum, then tilted his head to one side, frowning.

'I know, pet,' he said, 'it's hard, moving away. But you know, houses are just made of bricks and sticks. It's up to us to try to turn them into somewhere we can be happy. What might make you feel okay here, for now, until it feels more like home?'

That's how I ended up with the BEST bedroom EVER, the attic bedroom, high in the eaves and with a view out the back garden down to the tree house Hal had built ready for me. That tree house, complete with a trap door and a real working light, and a rope and bucket I could lower down for supplies, was the envy of my friends. Sometimes it doesn't take a lot to make a child feel safe and happy and comfortable. A little time. A little understanding. A little kindness...

'A little tree house?' Hal asks now with a laugh.

'A little you,' I tell him.

I try to get on with a bit more packing, but the Steadman's man has thrown me, and every time I glance out the window, I can see that poxy sign stuck in the lawn. A break. I need a break.

I have a little wander around the rest of the house instead. I've done that a lot lately, pacing the threadbare carpets late into the evening when I know Hal's safely asleep and doesn't need me at his bedside. Now, I pop into each room, aimlessly opening drawers and cupboards at random. There's so much that needs sorting, and I make some notes in my head. Mum's crystal animal figurines, arranged on the shelf in the hall like a sparkly zoo, will need careful packing. I'll take those home. I don't think Hal will mind. They'll be a nightmare to dust all the time but I hate the idea of them ending up at the back of a shelf in a charity shop. The towels and sheets and bedding in the airing cupboard we can give to the homeless shelter. They always need that kind of thing. In a wardrobe in the spare room, there are stacks of puzzles, Ravensburger 1000-piece cityscapes mostly, with a few canal boats and cottages thrown in for variety. I pick one up from the top of a pile and wipe away a layer of dust from the picture. 'Tower Bridge at Sunset'. I smile. Hal's always had a puzzle on the go, for as long as I can remember. He used to spend hours every evening, sitting quietly at the dining room table while Mum watched the telly or took herself to bed with a book. Often, in my late teens, I'd come home in the early hours and there he'd still be, eyes squinting, nose pressed almost against the cardboard, quietly fitting the pieces together.

'You didn't even notice me come in most of the time,' I tell him. 'I'd sneak past and up the stairs, so you wouldn't know how drunk I was, and then I'd listen to you come up not long after, relieved I'd gotten away with it.'

'Yes,' he says, 'that's exactly how it went.'

The puzzles will have to go. Even before things got rough, Hal's eyes were deteriorating. That's partly why I gave up my job and started coming round every day to care for him: making his lunch, doing his housework, staying over most nights too, if he needed me. There was no way I was letting him go into a home if I could help it. I knew he'd hate it, playing bingo in a hall that smelled of wee while Glenn Miller played in the background and someone brought him a plate of instant mash, undercooked vegetables and dry fish. Not. Happening.

'It wouldn't have been like that, Jen, love,' he chuckles, 'but I've always been glad to have you around.'

Back downstairs, I make another to-do list. Hoover the living room and the stairs, wash the windows, clean out the shower, dust the windowsills. I haven't been on top of those things recently. In fact, I've been letting everything slide since the notice arrived from the council saying the house had to be sold.

'Can't wait to get their hands on the money,' I grumble, glaring balefully at a case full of books in the hall waiting to be packed or donated.

'I know, love,' Hal says. 'Still, you'll have to make an effort, I'm afraid. They'll want to hold viewings, won't they.'

He's right, of course. I'm not going to let them straddle their high horse and say we're making things difficult. Though I suppose that ship sailed when I chased away the last Steadman employee who tried to stick up a 'For Sale' sign in Hal's garden. Ran after him, waving a rolling pin like a caricature of a madwoman, didn't I! Hal tried to stop me, of course – *Leave it, Jen! It's not his fault, you daft mare!* – but I wasn't ready to listen to him then, no way. I've calmed down since. Had to, really. They sent the police round to have a word, an older chap with a stern frown but kind eyes and a youngster with a pockmarked face, and I was told in no uncertain terms that I had to let the estate agents do their job.

'It won't make a difference, love,' the older chap had said, 'you'll still need to vacate the premises.'

Like I didn't know that already.

I go back to the kitchen and make some more tea. Two mugs, one weak with two sugars, one strong with none. Hal is sweet enough, or so he insists. I pop the milk back in the fridge and close the door. It's covered in magnets, the fridge. It was Mum's thing, buying a magnet from every place we visited to remind us of how much fun we had together on our adventures. Some of them are cheap and tacky, like the big plastic lobster with wiggling claws from Cornwall, while others are little ceramic works of art that track our movements around the world. There's one from Brixham, where we stayed in a tiny flat on the harbour, and Hal took me crabbing while Mum bought us ice creams from the shop. Another from Paris, where the three of us climbed the Eiffel Tower at dusk and I couldn't see properly so Hal lifted me up to see the lights stretching out in twinkling trails through the city below. My favourite, though, is a little Spanish lady in a black and red dress, caught mid-twirl with her castanets raised high above her head and 'España' written in glossy letters at her feet. My first ever holiday abroad.

'I was so scared of flying,' I say, reaching out to run my fingers over the Spanish lady's dress. 'I sat between you and Mum, and you each held one of my hands and got me through it.'

'You were always going to be okay, pet,' Hal says. 'You just needed a little encouragement.'

I let my hand drop to my side. A car passes by outside and water drips steadily from the tap into the sink as I sit down at the table and drink my tea.

'You know, we really should have a think about what to do next,' Hal says eventually. 'It's no good waiting till the last minute.'

I collect up the mugs – one empty, one full – and open the dishwasher. Damp, stale air wafts out, a testament to how long it's been since it was last used. I shove in the mugs and slam it shut again.

'What would make you happiest?' Hal asks and just like that, I'm back on the doorstep once again, a little girl lost as the world changed around her. I clench my fists.

'Easy,' I tell him. 'You come home. You remember who I am and you do your puzzles and read your books and you don't fight me while I try to dress you, or ask me one hundred times a day where Mum is, or why you can't go to the shops on your own.' I clench my fists. 'The nurses don't say you're better off somewhere else, and the government don't take your home to pay for that somewhere else. I look after you for as long as you need me to.'

I look down at the table.

'I'd like that too,' he says with a sigh, 'but we both know that's not possible. So what would make you feel okay?'

A bedroom in the eaves, painted my favourite colour and lined with posters? A tree house long since abandoned and dismantled?

'You are safe,' I say, 'safe and cared for for the rest of your life. I come to visit you. Every day.'

'Well,' he chuckles, 'it doesn't have to be *every* day, pet. You have to have a life too, you know.'

I bite my lip hard, so it hurts.

'I just thought you'd be coming home,' I say.

And that's the crux of it. When I surrendered Hal, just for a few days' respite, I thought he'd be coming back. I mowed his lawn, I changed his sheets, and I left his puzzle, half-finished, out on the table. Then he fell out of his bed and broke his hip, and the months passed by, and now here we are. The house will be gone and the hope with it, because you can't come home when there's no home to come to.

'Well, that's a bit dramatic, pet.' I can almost see him rolling his eyes. 'We'll be okay, you and I. All this, it's just… bricks and sticks.'

I glance out of the kitchen window. The sun is setting, turning the clouds pink. There's another question Hal likes to ask when he knows I'm struggling, but he isn't here to ask it, of course. He's in a hospital bed, five miles down the road, and has been for a while. I sit with him every day for as long as I can, and even though he doesn't always know my name, he *always* holds my hand.

I ask the question of myself instead.

'How can I make the best of things?'

I'm not sure, that's the answer. I'm not sure but I think I know where to start. I'll apply for some work, part-time of course, so I still have time to see Hal. I'll carry on sorting out his house, finding things familiar to him that will make his transition to the home easier. Maybe take him some old records so he isn't stuck listening to Glenn Miller all the time. I wonder if they'll let him do puzzles, if he wants to. If he can. I can ask if they've got anywhere for him to stick his magnets. If not, I'll take them and put them on my fridge at home, even the tacky plastic lobster! And undoubtedly packing away my childhood home, the best home I ever had, will shake more memories free. I can share them with Hal when I visit, remembering for both of us.

I glance out of the window at the sign on the lawn, wavering in the breeze.

'Bricks and sticks,' I tell myself as I get back to work.

'That's right, love,' I hear Hal say. 'Bricks and Sticks.'

Second to Last Rites
after the *Discworld* novels

Ruairi Bolton

When someone is going to die, you call for a physician. When someone is dead, you call for a priest. But when someone is dying – making their way, as they always do, into the world between life and death, where it is so easy to stumble in the dark and lose your way – you call for a witch, so they can perform the vital, gentle act of the Second to Last Rites.

It had grown late, with shadows pressing in as the children inched their way further up the mountain towards a light in the distance. They looked at that singular light with more trepidation than they'd ever shown the dark, even as mounting walls of it continued to surround them. All the dark could ever do was make the light that much more pronounced.

They edged closer, entering the farmstead: a smallish, homely province overlooking the countryside as it unfurled back down the mountain. The trees rustled in their clusters, emitting ominous, gossipy whispers, and the goats that'd yet to fall asleep bleated from their shelter.

In the centre of everything was the cottage, in which, through the porch window, the light flickered.

The children cast their eyes back longingly down the mountainside, the vantage granting them a perfect view of

Brisselrim, the place where the people lived – a village spotted with buildings built precariously around the rocky protrusions that speared from the mountainside. It shone with a domed glow.

It took them minutes to pluck up enough courage to knock on the door. *Her* door. A door so old it looked like it might disintegrate from the lightest graze. A door that was fracturing from the outside in, with splintering ravines like wrinkles running distances perpendicular to its edges. A door belonging to a cottage so well-kept and so long-living that it'd outpaced some of the most historic architecture they knew of.

Despite this, to their unspoken surprise, it managed to remain standing, sustaining the knocking with a resilience that somehow, in their minds at least – because to the logic of a child it was only natural that everything possessed feelings – made the entire structure appear surly and unremitting against the wear and tear of outside forces. It was like an old codger at the end of their tether, but one that'd been like that for a long time, strategically renewing their grip and holding on for just a little longer each time, unwilling to drift away. Not yet.

Movement stirred from within, the sound of heavy clunking boots reverberating off the floorboards, getting louder and closer.

The children had all been assured by adults that'd refrained from accompanying them that witches didn't really eat children, not *really* – the house looked far too savoury for that – but they all still had their doubts. Cannibal or not, they had never met anyone as scary as Agony Aunt Audrey.

There was a weighty sort of sound as the latch was unbolted and the knob began to turn, the movement drawing all the children's attention. They converged into a protective huddle, a wobbling mass of furtive glances and apprehensive gulps.

The door creaked in the appropriate way old mysterious

doors are supposed to (it was something of a veteran in the art) and groaned slowly open. A transient wall of what looked to be sheer gloom, though the children were as of the current moment uncertain as to whether this was merely their eyes playing tricks on them, lingered in its place before quickly dispelling, peeling off and away from a gaunt figure deeper within. Aunt Audrey appeared on the other side.

The candlelight outlined her as a looming, featureless silhouette, giving her traits like that of a great black buzzard on the porch. This seemed thematic considering the predatory glint to her glare – a violet, laser-accurate, gimlet gaze so infamous it was rumoured to be capable of engraving epitaphs onto exposed stone.

Her already narrow eyes narrowed some more to give each child a sharp appraisal. Based purely on her facial expression, there was precisely no indication that she was impressed with any of the conclusions she drew.

'What?' she asked.

There was a long silence in which the only thing the children did was shiver.

'*Well*?'

Another shorter pause, but this time it ended with the eldest receiving a sacrificial nudge. They stepped forward.

'M-miss Aunt Audrey, Miss. I-it's our granny…'

'Wait,' said Aunt Audrey, squinting. 'You're Anathema Gerkin's lot, ain't youse?'

A flurry of nodding heads.

'I see,' said the witch darkly, reaching back into the house to pluck her cloak from a nearby coat rack. 'Let's be off, then.'

The journey back down to Brisselrim was made in uncompromising silence.

The children looked scared out of their wits. Privately, Aunt Audrey found this to be gratifying. It was comforting to know that the reputation was still going strong, sinking deep into the minds of yet another generation.

In reality, there wasn't really anything to worry about; nothing would happen to you in Aunt Audrey's woods unless she willed it, and she didn't mind children, not *really*. That is, of course, if they were well behaved or, better still, absent.

The walk itself was familiar but taxingly slow for the old witch. Everything ached now. It all still worked, mind, but it'd been working for a long while. She tried to hide it despite stumbling a few times, explaining it away with mumbled excuses about loose stones and what not – just loud enough so that the children could hear – before pressing resolutely forward.

They travelled to Anathema's cottage, an insignificant little place on the outskirts of town. The parents were waiting outside. The mother had been crying, but feigned a very well-polished smile as soon as she caught sight of Aunt Audrey.

'Oh, Auntie.' Her voice was small. 'Thank you for coming.'

The witch brushed past her. 'Is she inside?'

The woman moved to keep up with her.

'Oh, yes. She's not doing…' She fell silent and made an effort to swallow.

Aunt Audrey hesitated, came to some internal decision and gave the mother a glance. Women can say a lot when it comes to glances, and witches could pack entire tomes in the space between eye and lid, so it stands to reason their looks alone were less like messages and more like encyclopaedias.

This glance said quite plainly in a calm, steady voice with little time on its hands: *I know you've been a mother for such a long time now. Time enough that you forgot what it felt like to be someone's child. But now you're remembering. And now it hurts.*

But when she spoke all she said was: 'I know.' She turned away. 'You – Dad.' She jabbed a finger.

The father straightened. 'Yes, Auntie?'

'Take the children home, now,' ordered the witch before she then made her way to the cottage. 'It's late and they'll need sleep.'

'Of course,' said the mother, beginning to herd them all away, father included.

Aunt Audrey paused right before reaching the door, her hand shaking over the knob.

'Um,' she uttered with uncharacteristic unease.

The family stopped and stared at her. She sighed.

'I would make sure that you say goodnight to her. Before leaving, that is.'

The mother swallowed. 'Yes. Yes, of course. Thank you, Auntie,' she said, shooing the father and her kids onwards.

Aunt Audrey stepped aside to let the woman pass, waiting by the front door until she reemerged. She thanked the witch upon leaving and, before doing so, said goodnight to her as well.

Aunt Audrey hesitated, pausing for a moment and watching as the woman left. After a while she gave a terse cough and said: 'Yes. I expect so. Soon, too.' She grunted and shook her head and made for the door.

Aunt Audrey stepped into the house and went straight to the bedroom. It was a simple and tidy affair, with minimal decoration and a straw-filled bed. In that bed was Anathema, who was small and frail and wrinkly, with a face like an overripe satsuma.

'Hello, Anne,' said Aunt Audrey from the doorway. She loomed there for a bit like a shade.

Recognition visibly fluttered in Anne's owl-like eyes and her mouth stretched in slow motion into a grin.

'Oh,' she said hoarsely. 'Oh, hello Audrey.'

Aunt Audrey nodded and walked inside. From there she did nothing much in particular, and continued to do nothing for several long minutes afterwards. Time ground by. As a pair they existed in quiet adjacency for an unclear period of time. A thickening of the atmosphere had taken place and a seemingly unbreachable silence swiftly settled in.

Aunt Audrey drifted around the space, observing and inspecting various items with an air of perfunctory aloofness, pointedly avoiding Anne's gaze.

And then Anne spoke, which rather spoiled things in the witch's eyes.

'I don't s'pose,' she said, her words ponderous and slow-moving, 'I have to call you Auntie, do I? You don't mind Audrey, do you?'

Aunt Audrey made no response, distracted by her inquisition into the woman's personal belongings, peeking into drawers and rifling through documents and noting the jewellery. She had no purpose in mind for any of it, just a standing curiosity.

'But I don't want to seem ungrateful. I *am*. It just takes some getting used to, I s'pose.' Pinching the edge of the covers, Anne looked sadly into a corner. 'I remember when it was your daddy that did these sorts of things. Should have seen it coming, really, but funny that it's you now. We grew up together.'

Aunt Audrey gave this some thought.

'We grew up alongside each other,' she said finally, sitting down and picking up a children's picture book. A few other volumes lay haphazardly on a shelf on the wall, but they looked a bit thick and lofty, with no pictures, and Aunt Audrey couldn't read.

111

'It's tonight, isn't it?' said Anne quietly. 'It happens tonight.'

Aunt Audrey looked at her. She did that for a long time before speaking. 'Yes.'

'Is there anything I can do?'

'Shouldn't think.'

'Is there anything you can do?'

'Probably.'

'Will you do it?'

'No.'

'I see.' Anne took some time to digest this, a heaviness in her eyes. She sank a little bit deeper into the bedcovers, as if some small flicker inside had finally died out and she had committed herself entirely to the spot she lay in.

Aunt Audrey leaned a fraction closer, interested to see the woman's next move. She wasn't a woman that made a habit of telling lies bold facedly; she merely told as much of the truth as she wanted and waited to see the conclusions people drew themselves.

Then Anne spoke: 'I understand. I know you have your reasons, and I know in my heart of hearts that they aren't cruel. You're not a cruel woman, Audrey. I know that much. And I won't turn away from your honesty. If you won't save me, it's probably because you shouldn't.'

Aunt Audrey nodded. 'It's a bad habit for witches to start testing the limit of what they can and can't do. Ends… wickedly, it does,' she murmured. 'I can't break no rules for you, but I will do something.'

She set the picture book down, walked over and, to Anne's amazement, knelt by the bed. The image alone would have made anyone that knew her gawk in astonishment.

It was like being waited on by royalty – more than that, even. Royalty were people, glittery and gilded but, at their core, human to every fault. They had the capacity to wait. Witches were earth, they were rock and stone – the jagged, unsightly things that somehow amounted to rolling meadows and mountaintops and things. They didn't bow to anyone.

But then Anne gave it some thought and realised that, in the flow of time, the only thing earth did was wait, just not usually on people.

Then Aunt Audrey took the old woman's hand – it was sallow and weightless – and simply said: 'I will stay with you.'

Tears began to form in Anne's eyes.

'Thank you,' she said. 'I don't want to be alone. Not tonight.'

'You won't be.'

They stayed in that position for a long while, chatting mundanely until Anne could get herself under control. They spoke furtively, like they were the only two people in the world. They spoke of old, old memories, both good and bad, stifling giggles and sobs alike as if they were worried they'd travel for miles. The world had become a sweetly gentle place, and they longed not to disturb it.

'I knew this was coming,' said Anne, 'sooner or later. It was your daddy that stayed with my family until their passing. My granny and grandad. And then you did my mum. Thank you for that. I'm happy that you came down here for me. I was scared you wouldn't.' She hesitated and then smiled. 'I almost forgot I made you something – t-to say thank you. Go – go. Over there.' Anne made a feeble gesture to the corner of the room. 'It's in the chest. Over there.'

A significant part of being a witch is thriving off the little gifts and offerings that the community gave to you out of habit (if they knew what was good for them, that is), and Aunt Audrey was as good a present exploiter as they came. She returned to her cane and hobbled over to the chest. She opened it and held up what she found and watched it unfurl until it hit the ground.

'I've been knitting for weeks now,' said Anne. 'Thought I might put myself to some use whilst I'm not going anywhere.'

'Oh,' said Aunt Audrey. 'Hrm. Ah. Thank you.' She looked at the garment for some time. 'It's...' Her brow wrinkled. 'Red's not really my colour.'

Anne didn't appear to be listening – her sweet little old lady factor was getting in the way. 'I just thought it's getting awfully cold these days and you must freeze up on that broom of yours. And you wear so much black too – I thought it might liven your day up a little.'

'Because I'm a witch, Anne. I wear black cos it's the colour a witch wears. It's like the whatsit called – uniform. And I don't need "livening up". I'm precisely as alive as I mean to be.'

'It was the best way I could think of to show my gratitude,' said Anne.

'The thought is appreciated but I don't think I can use a jolly red scarf.' Conjurations barged their way uncomfortably into Aunt Audrey's brain, images of her flying about on her day to day, dark imposing specimen of nature as she was, with a flapping, apple-red scarf trailing flippantly behind, rosy-cheeked children pointing and giggling up at her, parents looking from afar talking about how 'there goes the merry old witch'. She flushed. 'It ain't proper. People'll say things.'

'Do you knit at all, Audrey?'

'No.'

She scrunched up the scarf and tucked it deep, deep away in the recesses of her cloak. She didn't doubt she could make some use of it: bedding for the chickens or wall insulation or something. Witchcraft was called a craft for a reason, and another word for crafty was resourceful, which it paid to be when you weren't paid.

She settled down into an armchair by the bed.

'It's not personable with witchcraft,' she continued. Her mind quibbled briefly as to the strictness of the definition of personable. Aunt Audrey's resourcefulness famously extended as far as her choices in words, bending them into definitions they'd otherwise never have been able to experience. When you had a small lexicon, it paid to recycle.

She skewered the word under a spotlight in her mind and eyed it meaningfully. The definition promptly changed, doing the smart thing and shaping up sharpish to suit her needs. (In Aunt Audrey's world, which in her mind was the only one that really, truly existed, there was no such thing as a malapropism; it was all just a matter of word versatility. There was no more literal version of a wordsmith.)

The end result was to recontextualise the subject into a diorama exhibiting two figures locked in conflict – on one side there was witchcraft, on the other was knitting.

There was a philosophy that came with being a witch – well, more an attitude since witches didn't really go in for the big questions on life – and Aunt Audrey was absolute in her certainty that it didn't get along with the type of philosophy, if one was engendered even at all, of knitting.

'Bit of clothes-making is all well and good, but anything else is too much sitting about not getting much done for my liking,' she said, before looking sheepish for a nanosecond. 'No offence to the bedridden, mind.'

'None taken.'

'You didn't have to though,' said Aunt Audrey. For the most part this was true, but it was not the same as saying that she shouldn't. 'The Second to Last Rites ain't an honour, it's a duty.

I always say that though I can't do everyone, I'll do anyone, and that's something that can't be shaped by bribes.'

Course it didn't hurt your standing much neither, she thought.

Witches couldn't be moved with bribery, at least not very far, but it could certainly pique interest. It would never bend a witch out of shape though, not a proper one, not like it does with other people.

Ethel used to explain it as a good force, bribe-taking, Aunt Audrey contemplated. *By taking the money and doing nothing different, she'd be doing something good by making certain the bad men had less money to do other bribes with. It would only be an unexpected, happy piece of fortune that she'd come out the whole thing jammy rich. Not that I'd ever try something like that – I do witching properly, o'course. But she was a good one, Ethel, it has to be said. She did things her own way and what's more witchy than that?*

Then a sobering truth reintroduced itself to Aunt Audrey's mind and she wilted into her chair.

She… used to, anyway.

'Are you ok, dear?' asked Anne. 'You seem… tired. You're a stronger woman than me, but you're just about as old.'

Aunt Audrey sniffed. 'Comes with being a witch, I should think. You're a different kind of old. Sturdier.' She scratched under her chin philosophically. 'Prolly all the warts. Same typa logic of when you puts nails in a plank of wood – makes it harder.'

'I see,' said Anne, nodding.

A silence descended between them, and the vacuum their conversation left began to lure out all the quiet noises of the night. A miniature orchestra of the unobtrusive sounds, usually so easily pushed away, took their chance to close back in and take centre stage. The furniture creaked, clicks and scratches emitted like inconstant drumbeats, and the wind sang off key.

Aunt Audrey sat through it all, beleaguered, feeling as if the vacuum was also pulling at something inside of her, something she'd rather keep hold of. But this was demonstrative of a fundamental error to the understanding of how a vacuum operates. It wasn't being pulled, it was pushing. It didn't like the silence.

'It's… difficult,' ventured Aunt Audrey, her voice strained.

'What is, dear?'

'Watching you go. And not in the normal ways, I mean.' Aunt Audrey's expression wrestled with itself. 'I've watched lots of people die – plenty old and some young. I've seen good deaths and I have seen bad deaths, and I sometimes wonder which stays with me more. I ain't never killed before, but I've made it happen, and, if I am to be truthful just this once, my remorse ain't never let me let it go. But every single one of them was easier than this.'

Anne looked shocked. 'I never knew that you had such an attachment to me.'

'It's not that.'

'Oh.'

'Uh, sorry.'

'No, no, it's alright. I understand.'

'Right.'

'But then what is the matter?'

Aunt Audrey glowered a little, not quite believing she was letting the truth be squeezed out like this. 'You were in my life, Anne. From the beginning. All those other people, they were different histories – ones behind me. I go into the village sometimes now and see new faces, and I…' The faintest panic watered the edges of her voice. '…I can't remember if I've seen them before.' She took a moment and calmed. 'It's just coming to a head, is all. My history is dying. Standing here with you,

117

being here with you, in your room, surrounded by all the precious things of your life, it's like watching pieces of me be washed away. Soon I'll be the only one left with my memories.'

'Well,' said Anne after a while. She was at a loss for anything proper to say, so she just settled with saying: 'Sorry to be inconvenient,' in a slightly moody tone.

The two looked at each other and held each other's gaze, Aunt Audrey with a minutely shamefaced expression. Then, from the urging of some imperceivable cue, they started to cackle, Aunt Audrey taking Anne by the hand and rubbing it playfully.

Then the laughter subsided.

'Audrey,' said Anne eventually, her voice distant. It sounded like it was echoing from the bowels of a very deep cave.

'Yes?'

'I think it's close now.'

Aunt Audrey nodded. 'Yes.'

'Would you do something for me?'

'What?'

'Could you tell me about death?'

Aunt Audrey hesitated.

'Tell me anything. Please. Just put me at ease.'

The witch sighed. The appropriate time dreweth near, she supposed. She was fairly certain dreweth was a word. Close enough to one, anyway.

'Death,' she said. 'Let's see. Let's see. I think, above all... he's a bit of a lonely fellow. But nice once you get to know him. He is fair, and polite, dutiful and humane. He will take good care of you, mark that.'

'What's going to happen?'

'What will happen?' Aunt Audrey swallowed and readied herself to plumb the full extent of her vocabulary. 'When you close your eyes, he will be there. You will realise he has always been there. He will be there, and you won't be here no more. You'll be alone, save for him, our one constant companion. I urge you not to fear him. You can if you wish, if it makes you feel better. But don't misunderstand me, it will change nothing. I have met him many times, so I know. He will not be any less kind. He will come and take you closely and tell you everything will be alright and he will mean it. You will belong to a new world of night, where the eyes of azure flame will glide over you, and the stars will burn cold. He will wreath you in raiments of shadow, and guide you into the hereafter.'

Anne let the moment sit before saying anything. The lines hung in the air so vividly she could read them off the wall, and when she did, and she did many times, she felt a peacefulness rise through her. She stopped struggling and it all felt so small and easy, like falling asleep. She felt warm.

'Thank you, Audrey. That was beautiful.'

'Bloody well better have been,' sniffed the witch, making Anne laugh. 'Pardon my language but I put them tricky words in for a reason and I'd hate to see them go to waste.'

Aunt Audrey had specific opinions as to fancy words, ones that would lead some people into thinking that they might eventually run out. She only broke out the fine ones for special occasions. Words had power, and it would be nothing short of careless to just start throwing them about.

'It's like boots, I reckon. Good sturdy words I'm comfortable with. Maybe not the prettiest, but they get me from where I am to where I'm going. Save the big important ones, the sparkly ones with them enormous heels, for the important moments. Till then, you can rely on the old favourites.'

'I just use the ones I know,' said Anne.

'That's good too.'

'I only really have a few things left that I have to say, anyway. And I think one of them is goodbye.' She looked up at Aunt Audrey. 'I'm going to go to sleep now. I don't think I'll see you afterwards.'

'No.'

'Goodbye, Audrey.'

'Goodbye, Anne.'

Anne smiled and slowly closed her eyes. Aunt Audrey felt her grip go limp.

She waited in the dark for several minutes, just to make sure, and turned to something invisible in the shadows. 'Take good care of her.'

And from the shadows a voice answered. A voice as soft as cotton and as heavy as lead, that held in its core the iciest, quietest dark.

'I PROMISE.'

There was a great susurration, like the howling of microscopic storms, and a figure stood before her, scythe in hand.

Anne awoke and found herself in an askew, dreamlike parody of the world she knew. She could see Aunt Audrey, collapsed on her bed, still holding the hand of what now must be her body. She turned to look at the man beside her.

'Will she be alright?' she asked him.

'PERFECTLY,' he replied. 'I EXPECT SHE IS JUST A LITTLE FATIGUED.'

Anne looked around her. The world was fractal, edged in kaleidoscopic colours that bled into each other, giving her the impression she didn't quite have the right sort of eyes for this place. She looked up.

'She was going on a bit poetically, I think, but she wasn't kidding about those big flaming eyes in the sky, was she?'

'NO.'

'What are they?'

'THE DEATH OF DEATHS.' Death motioned for her to come closer. 'NOW, ANATHEMA GERKIN, I AM AFRAID WE MUST DEPART.'

'Oh dear, you can just call me Anne.'

'VERY WELL THEN, ANNE, IF YOU WOULD COME WITH ME.'

Anne gave a nervous laugh.

'Sorry, it's been a while since I've been able to walk anywhere, and now that I can, I'm scared stiff. I don't s'pose you'd be persuaded into taking my hand.'

'BUT OF COURSE,' said Death, outstretching a skeletal limb. She took it.

'Thank you. You're a very nice young man.'

'THANK YOU.'

'You're not very warm though, are you?'

'NO. I DO APOLOGISE. YOU WILL HAVE TO BEAR WITH ME. I AM STILL WORKING ON MY POST-PALLIATIVE CARE.'

'One of my grandsons would take me on walks, back when I could still stand.'

'THAT'S NICE.'

'You remind me of him.' Anne considered Death rigorously. 'A bit.'

Death tilted his skull, a bit like how a dog would turn their head, indicating that if he had a face it'd be emulating an expression.

'WHAT AN UNFORTUNATE STATE OF AFFAIRS FOR THE BOY.'

'Where are we going, if you don't mind? Anywhere nice?'

'I LIKE TO THINK SO.'

And they strolled serenely, hand in hand, to the Space Beyond Space.

Aunt Audrey woke up in the morning and realised she was drooling. She quickly wiped her mouth with her sleeve, looking around frantically to see if anyone else saw, before realising she was still in Anne's cottage. She tidied herself up before taking her leave, nodding to the undertaker – another veteran professional people seldom made small talk with – as he made his way up the road.

From there, she moved a short distance before pausing to stand in the cold morning air and considered something.

'I s'pose it is rather chilly out,' she said before extracting Anne's scarf from the depths of her cloak and wrapping it around herself. She examined herself briefly, noting the way the new accessory hung limply like a cloth caught in a tree, how it was already beginning to split-end, how much of the design was lumpy and off-kilter, and how much it all clashed with the rest of her practical, dutifully cared-for, non-frivolous attire. But, as mentioned before, it was a brief examination. She just had a very quick mind to take it all in, even in her old age.

'If this was what it came to after weeks of practice,' she said to herself, 'well, who knows, in ten years she coulda become half-decent at the thing.' She shook her head. 'Tsk, tsk. Don't badmouth the dead, Audrey. Not when you know so many.'

She made her way through the village to get to her farm, where, true to her suspicions, people stared. But then, she just stared back, which more or less solved the issue.

At some point, she found herself to be gripping the scarf. She rubbed the yarn with her thumb. She looked down at it. It felt warm.

Fish Market

Silvia Rose

'I have something to show you,' she said, touching his arm. 'I think it was around here… let me see.'

She dragged him by a bullish stride that managed to part thick sections of crowd – he was led as if through a cornfield – and noted with disappointment and a touch of shame that she had not turned to look at him once.

'Wait till you see this. You'll know exactly what I mean. I think you'll love it.'

But when they turned the corner she let out a gasp. 'Oh my god! It's gone!'

They stood in front of a building, its ripped-off facade crumbling white plaster, patterns of different-coloured tiles to mark the bathrooms on each floor – green, baby pink, mustard.

'It must have happened this morning. I was here yesterday, remember I told you…?' Her words tapered off in doubt.

He wanted to say, I believe you, but it seemed so trivial and obvious that instead he said, 'I would have thought a building like that would be listed.'

They stood staring at the autopsy before them – workmen in fluorescent jackets drilling into piles of rubble, like henchmen in some giant's barbaric meat carving.

It was lunchtime, or would be if they were home. The restaurant behind them was only just opening its shutters after a long lie-in.

A tour group passed, the guide inexplicably riding a segway. It felt like blasphemy, seeing such a comical machine glide over the ancient cobbles. The group stopped a few yards away, outside a doorway with stately cream-washed columns. Some museum, presumably, or perhaps just a post office if the town hall's opulence was anything to go by.

The guide went through his script, all the punchlines perfectly timed so as to sound off-the-cuff, jovial. Martin cringed at his contrived tone of voice – and worse still, the crowd's complete ignorance of it.

There was contempt in his gaze as he looked on at the guide before him, leaning forward on his segway, his T-shirt betraying patches of sweat. *Twat*, he thought.

A voice barged into his daydream – 'Ehhh heh! Ehh heh, brother! Sister! How's it goin'?'

A homeless man stood before them wearing a zip-up Adidas jacket and cycling shorts. He had a full head of dog-fur hair and a long beard which hovered beneath his face like a wispy cloud. His skin was clay-brown and was blessed with that same smooth texture.

'My brother! A mighty fine day, yeehaaw!' he bandied, mistaking them for Americans.

Sarah turned to Martin (for the first time that morning), silently imploring him to take charge of the situation. He was usually good at dealing with strange situations, he had a knack for getting people off the scent. But to her horror she saw that he was smiling – laughing, even!

'Don't shoot! We're not Yanks!' Martin said, holding up his hands in mock surrender.

The homeless man cracked up with a tinkling wheeze, as if there were scraps of metal jangling in his lungs.

'Where you from, pardners?'

'We're from Oxford, England. You know it?'

God, how she hated the way his voice would change whenever he spoke to someone 'foreign'. As if the rising inflection would make him more easily understood. *Twat*, she thought, throwing a sweet smile across to them both. She would not be the prudish tourist, no, no, no. She would be jokey, she would be light.

'*¡Hola!*' she said brightly and immediately regretted it, washed over with that special shame you get when you're trying to impress a child and they see straight through your false gaiety.

The homeless man flinched and stepped back, as if he'd suddenly sensed danger. He tripped on the curb behind him, sending an empty beer bottle rolling down the street. This seemed to be his cue to leave, and they both watched as without a goodbye he ambled his way beneath the shaded canopy of doorways and storefronts.

Sarah turned to her husband and caught the faintest tail-end of words swallowed backwards. Was he about to call after him? What would he say? The arrogance! As if they were buddies!

Her thoughts darkened. It wasn't arrogance. It was desperation. Desperation to talk to anybody but her. Even a nutter off the street.

The tour group had dissipated; they were now alone. A terrible screeching came from the bowels of the mutilated building – a sickly metallic sawing that rattled the pavement, the fillings in their teeth.

Sarah noted the door they were standing by had become unhinged. Clearly this was one demolition too many.

***

Later that afternoon, in the apartment they'd rented from Paolo, a fashionable photographer in his thirties, they sat on the small balcony listening to the conversation that was travelling up from the flat below. It was an English man and a Latina woman (they settled on Brazilian) and it seemed they were new room-mates, judging by their tone (more relaxed than budding romance, more strained than friends).

'God I'd love a cigarette now, wouldn't you?' Sarah stretched her arms up like a cat in the sun.

'Hmm. I don't know. Now you mention it…'

'Whenever I'm on balconies I get the strongest urge. I don't know why. Do you think Paolo smokes?'

'No. Why?'

'Cos he might have some tobacco lying around. I don't know. In the drawer or something.'

'More likely to find poppers.'

'That'd be nice too, actually! Ha! Why not!? God, it's been ages, hasn't it? Since we, you know…'

'…had fun?'

'No! I mean… well. Yeah.'

They both laughed and turned towards each other. There was a shift in the air, a breeze came to them like a small breath, a suppressed giggle escaping through nostrils. The city lights were on to signal the end of the day, and they wavered and blinked as if reflected on water.

'There's no reason why we can't.' Martin's voice had the stretched quality of a train slowing down.

'Why we can't what?'

'*Have fun.*'

'You mean…'

'Why not? It's Saturday, isn't it? Everything's really cheap here, I bet. And wasn't there that law just passed? Decriminalisation?'

'Are you serious? You're gonna go up to some guy and just *ask*?'

'Yeah, why not?'

'Well, I hope you brought a different shirt. You look like a grandpa.'

'Hey, grandpas need drugs too!'

Sarah laughed, again, feeling a sudden warmth.

'Oh, fuck it. Let's do it.'

'Really?'

Her heart quivered a little but she willed it still.

'Come on, let's get ready!'

***

They went to a bar with a name close to 'Death'. It was number one on all the comparison sites and seemed to fit that sweet spot of being loved by locals and trendy enough for the British palate. All the reviews recommended booking in advance as it was often crowded, even on weeknights.

They walked quickly through the narrow streets, passing the main cathedral square, tucked-away fountains and the hollow-looking bakeries on every corner.

The bar was empty when they arrived, and Martin felt embarrassed that they'd rushed to get there.

To enter, you had to step down from the street, making it feel more contained – underground and safe. It was tiny, just a row of stools by the counter with a few tall tables squeezed next to the walls, then a steep staircase at the end of the bar, leading up to a mezzanine where, thanks to the guidance of their waitress, they were shown to their table.

The waitress smiled like dripping honey as she handed them their menus, which had been slotted into old VHS boxes. Sarah zoned out as she recited the specials and let Martin relish the chance to waggle his tongue around the language. She looked around at the assortment of taxidermy on the walls – a boar's head, mice, a huge pair of antlers over the door frame. There were also paintings, all by the same artist, of S&M style pin-up girls. How would she describe the place? Rockabilly. Red velvet. After hours. She was satisfied with their choice.

After the waitress had descended the stairs in a frill of laughter they were left alone with the empty tables. There was promise of company soon, however, as the bar was filling up beneath them. Their eyes darted around greedily, finally landing on each other. Sarah was struck by a gloopy, slightly sad appreciation for the man in front of her. *Her husband.* All the stress and resentment from the past few days seemed to glide off with every twang of the guitar from the speakers, every roar of the coffee machine, every owlish turn of his head (especially at the waitress, she presumed; she always could tell when he fancied someone). He looked young again; the sun had caught the tips of his hair so that he shone blond under the low-hanging lamp. She'd chosen his most youthful shirt – light-blue and white stripes on thick cotton, a rounded collar. He was good-looking, she sometimes forgot that. A good, strong jaw, generous forehead and cheeks. She wanted to say plastic – she meant broad, she meant clean.

The waitress brought them a bottle of local Rioja. Villa Campanada, 2014. Full-bodied, organic. A jug of water, and two beers to start them off. As Sarah initiated a *'¡Salud!'*, Martin cringed affectionately. From the other side of the table he was admiring her bare shoulders, glowing with her half-

Balkan-blood tan. The faint flirtation of bare nipples pressing through her gold crochet top.

He usually hated the way she would try to orchestrate memorable moments. She was like a memory junkie, there was never enough. Everything had to be so *significant*. But no, in this moment he looked at her watery eyes and placid smile and was deeply relieved to feel the animal stirring of desire below his stomach – something he'd stopped associating with her a long time ago.

They ordered ceviche served in a large clamshell, oily tortilla with juicy slices of chorizo, tomato and basil-leaf salad, the usual sides of olives and bread. They feasted quickly, noisily, not noticing that the bar downstairs had become so full that people were perching on the pavement steps outside.

The night continued with generosity, wrapping them in its warm, dark embrace. They were cocooned in conversation – about trivial things, and big, sentimental things, and she enjoyed his caustic humour, and he enjoyed her salacious cackle, and they even ordered dessert – *two* desserts! – a strawberry cheesecake and a chocolate brownie, which soon dissolved them into a chorus of 'Mmmm! Ahhh! Oh my *god*, this is good!'

Sarah pretended to protest when the bill came, replacing Martin's card with her own.

'Darling. It's on me,' he said, handing her back the bright orange piece of plastic.

'Well, if you insist…' she retorted, matching his suave tone. She was about to reach under the table and grab a hold of his knee, to suggest something naughty, fertile, some kind of game, when he said, 'I guess the goods are on you.'

'Hmm?' she said, startled. 'Oh. Yes. *The goods.*'

She felt her pulse quicken at the mention of the drugs. Her

mind sifted back through the filing cabinet of her youth, which threw out tantalising snapshots of lipstick, catsuits, the edges of sinks. The buzz, the arrogance, so on-edge – *devouring* the edge.

'Do you think we'll be able to find some?'

Her question seemed to pierce something with its mumsy rationality. She immediately chastised herself, wishing she could have played along in the bubble. She was even more disheartened to admit there was a bubble in the first place.

'Probably. We can just ask people on the street. Or the waitress!' His eyes widened at the prospect.

'True.'

Downstairs, a disastrous succession of breaking glass made the punters roar and cheer, as if someone had scored a goal.

Sarah went to pee and almost tripped over the step to the tiny, wallpapered bathroom. She felt her thighs spill over the toilet seat, caught the sour tang from her damp underarms – that familiar carousel of self-disgust. She imagined Martin trying to be subtle as he asked the waitress where to pick up. She could practically taste his syrupy tone.

And there he was, waiting outside holding out a cigarette like he'd bought a red rose. A wicked grin strewn across his face.

'Oh my god, I love you!'

'I would've bought a whole brick if I'd known that would be your reaction.'

'Ha, ha. I should be so lucky…'

They passed it back and forth between them, letting the harsh smoke course and cut their lungs in a delightful surrender to bad habits, the liberation of un-health. Both of them began noticing passers-by, sussing them out as potential leads. They were looking for someone between trustworthy and edgy – tattooed, attractive twenty-somethings being the ideal target.

The air was chilly – charged with pre-midnight adrenalin.

They stood still for a while in the same spot, Martin shifting his weight from one brown-loafered foot to the other, his eyes bearing all the concentration of a fisherman scoping out shore.

'¡Perdón!', his voice a lasso capturing the attention of a passing couple, their faces blank and curious. Sarah zoned out, studying the gaggle of homeless men perched outside a 24-hour bakery, which looked more like a walk-in vending machine, replete with a wall full of plastic display cases, an impersonation of choice.

Judging by the couple's quick descent down the pavement and Martin's unchanged expression, his pitch had not been successful.

'Come on. We won't find anything here. Let's walk around.'

They headed back towards the centre through the side-streets lit up pale gold, past arbitrary landmarks that only Sarah recognised – a florist called 'Sara', a shop selling door handles, a road sign that read, simply, 'Peace'. They reached the base of the big hill with the statue of Jesus, looming large and white, where only yesterday they had climbed its summit, pleasantly surprised at how uncrowded it was for such a notable landmark. They'd soon found out why, as they took shelter under Jesus's stiff robes, escaping the violent afternoon heat.

Now, there was a church to their left – on closer inspection it was a hotel with stately columns and diffused lighting which seemed to radiate off the building itself rather than from any particular fixture. Sarah pictured the rooms inside – white, padded, sparse, longing for their anonymity.

'Him?' Martin gestured to a man in chef whites, smoking a cigarette on the hotel steps. He sat with wide legs and stared aggressively into the night.

He paused before taking two long strides towards the chef. For the third time that day, Sarah zoned out as he flexed his linguistic muscles while trying not to look like she was a woman in her late thirties waiting for her husband to score.

'Any luck?'

'No, but he said we should go to this neighbourhood, sounds like "fish market". He said we should find something there, easy.'

'Right, OK. Is it far?'

The wine was wearing off slightly. Sarah observed the encroaching clarity with disdain.

'I don't think so. Come on, the night is young!'

She let his forced ennui flap desperately in the space between them, like a late summer wasp, neither of them having the energy to keep it from falling.

They began walking through streets that felt familiar from their daytime jaunts, yet now in darkness had turned. Their footsteps resounded on cobbles, conversations hushed as they passed, as if the streets themselves were housing an intimate dinner party, and they, the uninvited guests.

They stopped outside an expensive-looking bar lit up with gold bulbs, evoking images of blonde-wood interior and cocktails served in pickle jars. A couple stood outside – the man, podgy and bearded, holding up a pushbike; the woman, small and leather-clad, blowing reams of vanilla-tinged smoke from her e-cigarette.

Martin adopted his faux-casual fluency and began asking for directions, only to be cut across by the man, in perfect English, 'You guys on holiday?'

Sarah couldn't help but baulk at the sardonic edge to his question, the swagger with which it rolled out of his mouth. She knew Martin would take this switch in linguistic track as a gross display of power, and so edged a little closer to him, on his side.

'Yeah we are, actually, although I studied here. A few years ago now, mind! In Madrid. Not here. But close.'

'We're looking for the Fish Market?' Sarah cut in boldly.

'You mean Barrio de los Pescados?'

'I guess?'

'¡Sí, sí, eso!' Martin nodded. 'We're actually looking for, uh, you know…' He lowered his voice into the seductive tone of an accomplice.

The couple exchanged a glance and the man responded, 'Ah, I see. Sure. You will find something there, no problem. But be careful with your belongings, eh?' He tapped the pocket of his jeans; then, satisfied that they were taking him seriously, pointed down a dark street in a direction they hadn't been before, separate as it was from the main bulk of town.

They waved their thanks and continued on, the pavement empty, all of it so oddly numb, as if this neighbourhood had an early curfew and everyone was well asleep. The moon was more pronounced here and under any other circumstance Sarah would have stopped for a moment to swoon, and Martin would have rolled his eyes, but of course this was not any old circumstance: they were on a mission.

'Sod's law, isn't it? If this was Amsterdam…' Martin threw back his remark from five steps ahead.

Finally, a sign of life: from a side-street to their left came the faint hum of reggaeton and coarse, croaky voices. Two men sat on small fold-up deckchairs, legs spread, with cigarettes smouldering between their fingers. There was a thick printed

133

blanket hanging instead of a door, which let out a rectangular frame of yellow light and the impression that there were more of them inside. The men had a menacing youthfulness about them, though they must have been around Martin's age. They wore crudely coloured hi-tops and T-shirts with loud slogans. They stared up, amused as two leopards.

'¡Hola muchachos! Una pregunta – '

'¿Qué quieres? Wha' you wan'?'

'Buscamos algo. Algo…'

Smiles cut both their faces in half. Sniggers passed between them like handfuls of loose change.

'¿Puro? ¿Coca?'

'¡Coca! ¡Sí, sí!' Martin's raised voice betrayed his excitement. He repeated himself, but this time quieter, reining it in. 'Coca. Un poco. Para mi y mi esposa. Para nosotros. Es nuestra última noche y – '

'Vale, señor. Treinta euro por un medio.'

The younger-looking one of the pair seemed to be in charge of business. The other, bushy beard, low eyebrows, sat on a plastic drinks crate and had the presence of a loyal dog – watchful, in locked agreement.

The *jefe* called in to the house and out came a woman in her sixties, though she too had a strangely young appearance, as if they were all just a bunch of kids to whom the years had been particularly cruel. She wore a faded floral apron dress stretched tight across her sturdy bosom. White roots glowed beneath rusty copper dye in a defiant betrayal of her age. The scowl etched on her forehead seemed as comfortable as a well-trodden path – not put on especially for the strangers at her doorway, but more a permanent fixture.

After hushed instruction from the younger man (her son?) the woman went back inside by lifting the curtain-door, returning a minute or so later with a clenched fist and defensive gaze. The man beckoned to Martin, excluding Sarah from this tight, serious huddle, and it was too late now to voice the cold feeling of fear that seized her by the stomach. She looked around and saw nothing but the approaching early hours fill the empty streets like an odourless gas. A cat ran over a pile of rubbish and sent a tin can tap-dancing down the pavement and she thought of the homeless man from that morning and was filled with a strange nostalgia – a strange pining for an innocence which hadn't existed in the first place.

'OK?' Martin's command to leave, retrace their steps back towards the city, with the sounds of the men and their reggaeton as real now as a memory of a hallucination, or a thought.

It's always a bad sign when you know what you should do and how you should act so clearly, and yet can in no way make it happen, thought Sarah. If this were good, if I were happy, I would be grinning, I would be giggling, I would squeeze my husband like a child.

Instead there was silence. An unspoken urgency to get out of the neighbourhood as quickly as they had entered.

***

The stone bench was icy-smooth; the square deserted. Sarah and Martin sat mirroring each other, their legs dangling off opposite sides. Between them – Sarah's phone, its black surface sitting blank and serene. Martin dug into the tiny pocket of his jeans, usually reserved for condoms, and brought out a tight wrap made out of a takeaway menu. Inside its origami folds, white powder, like a quantity of salt you would dismiss as too much, perhaps a generous serving for three people if the meal was bland. He poured some on the screen with a look of pure concentration. Sarah wondered if he could sense her nerves. They were, after all, so close, with only skin and air between them.

Martin herded the uneven powder into two short, stubby lines. Sarah watched his careful movements as she took a ten-euro note out of her purse and rolled it into a cylinder. There was the solemn silence of a ritual which made any outside noise come as an intrusion – the roar from a football audience, beeps and revs, the scuffle of pigeon claw.

Sarah inhaled first. The powder could, of course, have been anything, but in that moment it was imbued with build-up, hope, expectation – and oh, oh, there it was – that familiar sting of numbness, smell of chalk and petrol, the semi-immediate rush down that mysterious channel behind the nose, at the top of the throat, to the spine, to the toes.

'Weeeehooo!' Martin screeched, grimacing as if he'd taken a shot, which he had, in a way. 'Nice stuff, eh?'

Sarah nodded, unaware that her jaw was clenched. She was excited. Now they could – now it would be – now – *now what?*

'We could…'

'We could what?'

'I don't know. What should we do?' Sarah put her hand on her husband's jean-covered thigh. The material was thick and compact, so much so that he barely felt her attempt at a squeeze. 'Ummmm…' She rubbed harder, trying to catch his eye, but he continued to face away, lost in a shadow that sliced across half the square.

He abruptly stood and held out his hand. 'Come on,' he said, gripping her palm.

'Wait a second, we have to clean this up. Wait, Martin!' she hissed, scrabbling to wipe the phone screen and stuff the note and card back in her purse – the evidence.

But Martin did not wait. Already he was descending down the dark artery of a side-street, causing Sarah to half-run in pursuit.

'You know what I'd love?'

'A cigarette?'

'Well, yeah, but no – an *espresso martini*.'

'You're full of new ideas today, aren't you?' He did not stop or even turn around to acknowledge her request.

'I haven't had one for years. It's my favourite cocktail, you know,' she addressed to his back.

'I remember.'

'Coffee, dessert, alcohol, all in one. What's not to like?'

There were isolated aspects to the moment that pleased Sarah. The cut-glass clarity of her vision, the tingling down her neck, the dreamy-lit buildings, the promise of cocktails and the sprawling night ahead. All these aspects – precious as treasure, and yet they seemed to her like items from a jewellery box floating without gravity, further and further apart – beautiful in themselves, but where was the body to bring them together?

Martin spotted the flashing lights of a plane up above and wondered where it was headed. He liked to play this game with himself and with the aid of his app, he was able to gauge the direction and was even now getting well-versed in the different airlines and their routes. Under his prediction this was an EasyJet flight, Gibraltar to Manchester, possibly London. He pictured the passengers suspended in their seats all those miles above (7.2, on average) and envied their state of sleepy transience, their surrender to the in-between. Their route on pavement, towards a bar to drink another relic from Sarah's catalogue of nostalgia, seemed to pale in comparison.

After a series of dead-ends and attempted lures into tacky

nightclubs, they were promised an espresso martini in one of the swanky bars which lined the central avenue. Voluptuous bass pulsed out of the speakers; slick-haired, waistcoated bartenders shook metal tumblers with bored eyes. It wasn't the kind of place they'd usually go to but it seemed to fit the general theme of the night – out of ordinary, decadent. As they waited for their drinks they took each other in, exposed once again in over-the-table proximity, their faces appearing now in high definition, the cocaine buzz silence like a blanket of snow over the heady murmurs of their fellow punters – statuesque women with long, languid limbs and their pot-bellied companions.

Martin reached out to hold Sarah's hand, a gesture so out of character that her first instinct was that it was some kind of joke or warning. But no, in his eyes inexplicably rose two pools – he squeezed her hand – 'We've had a nice time, haven't we?' he said in a small voice.

Unsure whether he meant the holiday or their marriage she simply said, 'Yes', and smiled, and she meant it, she thought, in that moment.

'Remember when we first met? We used to have those breakfasts…'

'Yes of course! I made the guacamole, cut the tomatoes— '

'And I made the eggs. And the milkshake.'

'Funny how when you're in a routine you spend the whole time wishing you weren't in it, terrified of boredom, and yet you have no idea how precious those routines are. How fleeting.'

Sarah worried that she'd gotten too sentimental, that he'd be put off, retreat, but he continued gazing at her with a distant fondness, nodding in the way that a distinguished scholar would nod at a particularly bright, promising student.

'I've always thought we're similar, you know. At least back then. Just doing our own thing, not giving a shit. You always—'

Two glasses landed in the space between them, the waiter's starched white arm arranging them precisely to the right of their shoulders.

'Excuse me? Is that an espresso martini?'

The waiter stared blankly. 'Is martini.'

'No, I ordered an *espresso* martini. With coffee? Vodka?'

'No. We have only martini here.'

'OK. OK. Just leave it. No problem.'

Martin had ordered a Moscow Mule and she gazed at the tall glass with envy, frosted and overflowing with fresh mint and ice. Her (regular) martini sat cold and clear and still, with a single nonchalant olive bathing at the bottom.

'Fuck's sake! After all that searching! … No. I mean, it's fine. It's fine.' She took a sip and grimaced against the medicinal bitterness of an honest mistake.

***

To their dismay the city seemed to be winding down by three a.m. It was a relatively small city after all, but still, they had half-hoped for an endless string of bars and clubs, refill upon refill of the local nocturnal *zestiness*. Instead it seemed they had outstayed the party. They were practically swept from the streets by the intimidating mass of garbage trucks.

After a good twenty minutes of fervent striding, and a few pit stops in between, making use of Paolo's keys, they arrived at a playground. They'd walked up a long pedestrian stretch that ran next to a motorway leading out of the city. Outskirts – imbued with that particular lack of name or character, for which it seemed to compensate with a smattering of billboards and brands, logos, advertisements for cut-price sportswear, toothy grins from a private dentist's, posters for a circus passing through. The sleepy glow of a supermarket closed.

Everywhere, signs.

What made this patch a playground was the sandpit and the swings, and perhaps the concrete spheres that lined the avenue. The ground was black and spongy, a gentle child-friendly kind of tarmac. Without a word they each sat in a swing and began rocking back and forth, gathering momentum. The chains felt heavy and final, and Sarah was reminded of those times swinging so high she thought she might go loop-de-loop, and of the way the tender skin of your inner arm would get pinched between the links if you weren't careful.

'Music?' asked Martin, already scrolling through YouTube. He chose, predictably, a German techno track which he had played non-stop during a brief foray into Djing, a period Sarah recalled with fond embarrassment. The track hammered and echoed into the still night. Such stillness, with a chill approaching, like the faint detection of something gone rotten.

Sarah opened her mouth and immediately forgot what she was going to say. There was nothing to say, in fact. Martin stared onwards, captivated, apparently, by the music.

Sarah felt that she might cry, were it not for the flood of apathy that had overtaken her.

Minutes passed.

No one came.

The music stopped, battery dead.

Sarah walked up to her husband who was still on the swing, foot still tapping to the beat fresh-gone. She kneaded her fingers at the base of his scalp where stubble turned to hair, lowered her lips to his earlobe.

'Time to go,' she said, her voice drowned out by a ship's horn in the distance, plaintive as a cow who'd lost its calf.

Kind Red Spirit

Ruby Burgin

Sakura's father had been unusually quick to bury his wife. Akari was buried three days before the gravestone's arrival. Against Sakura's plea for next-day, her father, Hiroto, clicked the cheaper standard delivery.

The package arrived before the school bus. Instead of catching the bus to school, Sakura took the train to the cemetery with her father. When Sakura had asked how her mother ended up in the cemetery, her father answered 'by train'. She wondered if her father meant it in a different way. Her stomach had plummeted the moment she stretched her small leg over that gap between platform and carriage, her mind backtracking to when her mother had said 'goodbye' and meant the truest meaning of the word. Sakura struggled to excavate the *good* out of her mother's parting word as Akari lay hidden under piles of dirt.

Hiroto stood in front of a mound with the boxed gravestone hanging in his arms. For all the physics that Sakura had learnt in class, she found it strange how the slab of stone refused to tumble out of her father's limp hold — like the weight of his world was hanging by a heartstring that had been tugged on too many times.

'She's here?' Sakura asked.

'She's gone.'

'She's here,' Sakura said, placing her hand on the mound of

upturned soil that had upended her family's life. Her small hand made the grave look even bigger. Her young mind made it even harder to understand how her mother had gone to the underground to visit Grandpa and now was underground in soil.

Her father opened the top of the box then flipped it over onto the border between untouched and upturned ground at the head of Akari's grave. Stamping down on it with a polished shoe, Sakura's father secured the headstone into the ground and ripped the box away revealing the two engraved names: Hiroto and Akari. A pot of red paint and a half-snapped paintbrush fell out.

He staggered back three paces, staring down at the gravestone, leaving Sakura to dip the half-broken paintbrush into the paint pot with a delicate hold; a splinter would only make this more painful.

She began to fill in the first character of her father's name with paint.

'Isn't it supposed to be the adult that does this?'

Her question fell on deaf ears. She guessed it made sense; once her father died, she would be washing this red paint off to signify that he had joined his wife in death.

'Why did no one come to her funeral?' Sakura asked as she started to fill the second character of his name, struggling to keep the splintered brush in her hand, her fingers slipping where the paint had snuck up during the messy work.

'No one knew she was going to die. She wasn't ill beforehand. She just decided to.'

How strange. 'How? If you can't choose whether to start living, how can you decide to die?'

'I don't know how.'

'Then why?'

'I don't care why,' he snapped.

Sakura dropped the paintbrush on the soil, leaving the painting unfinished and a dollop of red paint amongst the grass like a budding rose, red with loving wrath and littered with thorns, greedily reaching out for that prickling pain at the ends of curious fingertips. 'If you loved her, why are you angry at her?'

'I'm angry at what she did to herself. Aren't you?'

'I'm angry she's gone. *How* doesn't matter.'

'It's shameful,' her father hissed.

'That's not true!' Sakura began to cry and slapped the paintbrush. It spiralled across the ground towards her father's feet. The trail of blood-red paint connected the father and his daughter across the churned earth of Akari's grave. Fury blossomed; animosity bloomed.

Sakura ran and stormed into the girls' section of the cemetery's toilets. She filled the plugged sink with icy water, punching it with her paint-covered hands until the water was tinted cherry-blossom pink, ripples of red extending from delicate porcelain fists. Only the most stubborn of pear-shaped paint splotches were left to stain her hands.

The cubicle door creaked behind her. She lifted her eyes to the mirror nailed to the wall above the ceramic sink. Behind her, in the reflection, was Aka Manto.

Inches above the toilet, he floated, draped in his infamous red cloak, forming origami creations out of coloured toilet paper.

'Your hands.'

Sakura jerked at the sudden voice emanating from behind his pearlescent mask. The lips painted onto his mask did not move, so the young girl was unable to distinguish whether the spirit had spoken out loud or in her head.

143

Aka Manto gestured out a wispy arm towards her paint-spotted hands. 'Would you like some toilet paper to wipe it off? Red or blue?'

Sakura denied him an answer, not trusting herself to be cleverer than this too-clever spirit. If she uttered one wrong word, she might be killed. She dragged her hands across her charcoal-coloured school skirt instead.

The features of Aka Manto's white mask didn't move, not the hollow black eyes or the painted plump red lips, but he leant back as if in contemplation or shock that Sakura had outmanoeuvred his deadly question. He ripped off another square of blue toilet roll and creased it into a butterfly.

'Would you like it? Use it to wipe the tears from your eyes.'

Sakura pulled her white sleeve across her face as an answer.

'Why are you crying?' asked Aka Manto.

Sakura paused to think of a safe answer. '*Why* doesn't matter.'

'People only cry for what they lost or what they can never hope to find. Which one are you?'

'My mother died.' She had lost her mother; therefore, she couldn't find her ever again — so maybe she was both these people?

'You are crying for an absence, an uncharted part of the map, otherwise you wouldn't be lost here.'

'I'm not lost.' Sakura stomped to the exit and pulled on the door handle. Locked. No, it wasn't locked. How could something without a lock be locked? It simply refused to open for her. How strange indeed. 'This isn't real,' she declared.

'You're in Denial.'

'I'm not denying anything.' She pouted at the too-clever spirit for his blunder. 'I'm saying this isn't real. Just because something is unreal, it does not mean it is denied existence.'

'No. You are *in* Denial — the place — and you'll be stuck here unless you decide to move on.'

How could denial be a physical place to be stuck? 'How do I escape if this door won't open?' She pulled on the door another time and it rattled in the doorframe.

'You cannot go through a door that leads you backwards. You will have to use this door to move on.' Aka Manto pulled his red cloak aside to reveal a small door on the wall, only big enough to let a small girl crawl through. 'You will have to succeed in all of the tasks to survive Grief.'

'Grief?' she whined.

'It's the place beyond this door. If you do not complete all of the labours then you will remain there, stuck in time. If you refuse to go in, you will stay here, in Denial.' Aka Manto had made a second butterfly, this time with a square of red toilet roll, and held both out for Sakura to choose from, moving both hands up and down to make the tissue paper wings mimic a butterfly in flight. She turned from his silent deathtrap towards the small door and crawled through.

***

Sakura stepped out of the toilets in the north-east corner of Nijō Castle. She would have suspected that her encounter with Aka Manto had been a silly daydream, but the cherry trees were sad and the garden was empty despite it being tourist season in Kyoto. She tried to go back but, like the other door, this one would not open. She slapped the wood, kicked the hinges, bent over and roared at the handle until her breath blurred the varnished brass knob. Using her sleeve, she polished the handle until the orange-gold metal reflected a looming shape floating behind her.

'You are late,' the ghostly white spirit behind her said.

'How can I be late?' Sakura huffed, turning to face the woman. 'I wasn't expecting to come here at all. How do I leave?'

'You are not very patient.'

'You just chastised me for taking my time,' snapped Sakura.

The spirit sighed and floated around the trunk of a cherry tree, the fallen petals stirring under her as if they had been called to flight by a light wind, trailing her as if they were her shadow. 'I am Onryō. You must reach the set of toilets in the west of the castle grounds to escape this place.'

'All I have to do is get to the other side?'

'That is correct.'

Finally, something simple. Sakura knew the grounds well from days out with her parents to school trips. She headed west, but as she passed Onryō, the spirit plummeted and the garden rumbled. Cherry blossom trees lamented her fall and wept shell-pink tears. Sakura's legs sank to the shaking earth and she crawled amongst the trembling petals.

'You didn't tell me there would be an earthquake!'

'Life is unpredictable,' the spirit mused, her voice rumbling like oncoming thunder, relaxed in its inevitability.

Sakura staggered out of the garden and sped towards the weeping pagoda tree. Wind hit her back and threw her against the trunk of it. The gale shadowed Onryō as she circled Sakura until a tornado surged, whipping vines across Sakura's body. She shouted, spat, tore at the vines with her teeth, nipping her skin during the attack.

Freeing herself, she headed into Seiryu Garden, but each leaf and blade of grass became fire under her footprints. Sakura roared and raged forwards as the orange flames blossomed around her coal-black school shoes. The world was smoke and every tear that escaped her eyes heated into steam and joined it.

She slumped down into the lake in front of the teahouse, punching her blistered fists into the water to cool the burnt red splotches.

'This is impossible,' she growled. 'I'm so tired. I can't battle all these disasters.'

Onryō floated above the water in front of Sakura, the spirit's reflection melding into Sakura's rippled version. Curious. They looked so similar: flowing white sleeves, matted black hair, pursed lips.

'Have you given up?' the spirit asked, her red lips curling into a smile or a sneer that could be decided by a coin toss. Sakura no longer trusted her luck.

'Yes. I don't care if I'm stuck here. Moving forwards is just too difficult.'

'Congratulations,' Onryō said. 'You have passed.'

'I don't understand,' cried the young child.

'Sometimes giving up is the only way to move forward in the right direction, rather than raging forwards in the wrong one.'

Sakura looked down into the ripples of the lake and the orange light from the burning garden faded and spilt into the waters until everything around her, even the water, was molten gold. Onryō had faded from the water's surface, but something else had crept up over Sakura's shoulder with a menacing smile.

**

Shōjō swayed over Sakura's drooping shoulder in the reflection of the lake, his grin twisting in the ripples. She could feel a weight there, but it was not Shōjō. It was as if he was sitting on her shoulder instead of the crooked tree branch leering over her.

The grass blades of flame had grown like vines over an abandoned home. Their gnarled talons of red-tipped flames ripped through the buildings of Rokuon-ji temple, each touch turning ornately carved wood to charred beams that snapped with gold sparks of witchcraft. The only building they had not yet torched was the Golden Pavilion behind her, coated in gold leaf, reflected upside-down on the surface of the lake.

'There you are!'

Sakura's eyes followed where the sound had come from. Shōjō swung from a tree branch above her. He tilted his flat face too much, rotating it as if it was not attached to his short neck. How curious.

'Lose someone?' he asked, stretching out his orange-haired arm and a knobbly finger. Sakura thought he was pointing at her own heart, but as she glanced at herself, her eyes caught sight over her shoulder of the other side of the lake.

Across the water was a man whose distorted face was unrecognisable through the smoke billowing from the ignited buildings.

'I did lose someone, but not him,' Sakura said, pulling at the skin that had bunched around her red eyes. 'Please, I'll do anything to get out of here.'

'You? Do anything?'

Shōjō's smile rippled through his tough, calloused skin until it was nearly too big to fit his face. He floated down from his branch to the ground and stalked towards Sakura on hand-like feet and feet-like hands.

'I've lost my mother and now I fear I'm losing myself even more so than I already had,' Sakura admitted, pulling her hair.

A few strands gave up and curled around her fingers like rings, slotting comfortably into her tired skin. She pressed her bony hands against her retreating stomach and hollow chest. Everything was running away from her.

'I've got something you can take, a medicine to cure what you feel.'

Shōjō dipped his leathery hands into the lake and presented the golden water to Sakura in his wide palms. She opened her mouth and the spirit poured it down her throat. There was no need to swallow.

The liquid warmed her like a sunset, turning her thoughts and memories and skin into a summer haze. She was taking flight towards the sun. Weightlessness. She hung in an intangible equilibrium.

'I don't feel anything,' she said.

'It's working. But you must continually drink it to maintain the effect,' Shōjō said, gesturing to the man across the lake who dipped his empty glass bottle into the gold water.

Her feverish eyes darted over the water. Anything would be worth it to kill this grief. She'd drown herself in the lake if that's what it would take. No one could persuade her otherwise.

She dropped to her knees on the bank and drank the spirit's liquid until her pain distorted and slumped, too numb to keep her going. She collapsed into the lake with splayed arms and an open gullet.

Ballet dancers with seaweed hair and vines for arms twirled with the current's rhythm. They circled Shōjō on the bed of the lake. She hadn't noticed him follow her.

Foaming white bubbles collected around the dancers like her mother's wedding dress. There had been no photos of the wedding displayed in the house. Only once did she watch the tape of their first dance. There was a warped silence to the video. Their mouths moved, but the person holding the camera was too far away to capture the words exchanged. The only remaining evidence of a once happy wedding turned dutiful union.

Her parents twirled in the tape as they twisted each other's words in the kitchen. They danced around each other in a very different way, mimicking and mocking each other, marching on eggshells, burying and triggering landmine bombshells that could shatter Sakura's rose-stained glass world. She knew it was her father who had slammed the door hard enough to knock her mother's pottery off the shelf.

Firework bubbles exploded from above as the glass bottle smashed through the sky of Sakura's new underwater world to get refilled. The sodden label had wilted at the corners; white paper fibres detached and floated in the current. There was a three-tiered temple on the front, a Goban Golden Ale then, something native to the top shelf of her father's fridge.

Underwater, there was no smoke to cloud the stranger's hunched stature. Her eyes trailed the Goban's label to his ringed fourth finger, up to the face of her father. She opened her mouth to call to him, but molten gold had filled her lungs until there was no room for air.

This was no medicine, but she had believed Shōjō's lie so easily for the small hope it gave her.

She kicked her legs to swim up to her father, but the ballet dancers' vine arms had one of her legs and Shōjō's feet-like hands had her other locked in place. Reaching up, she grabbed the submerged Goban bottle from her father's hand and smashed it against Shōjō until the top broke off and Shōjō's hand retreated. Sakura grabbed the vines around her leg and used the broken bottle to carelessly tear through them and the skin of her wrists, drawing ruby streaks through the gold. Only for a moment did she check down to see Shōjō's grinning face in the murky depths at the bottom of the lake.

Her father's hunched and rippling body lay just beyond the surface of the water that was keeping Sakura trapped.

She resurfaced, climbing onto a bank not of a lake, but a river. Shōjō and the ballet dancers and the burning pavilion were gone, but so was her father.

***

Sakura stared into the Kamo River. Was it her journey or the ripples that had gifted her wrinkles? She looked like her mother, aged and tired despite her youth.

The river was shallower than usual. Her eyes started to cry without permission and hit the river's surface. The tears filled a transparent container of a man's body standing on the water and overflowed into the river. It resembled a wicked version of her mother, dressed in sea-foam white, with matted black hair and a ruby red tongue. He looked like the male counterpart to Onryō, the spirit of natural disasters that Sakura had left behind her.

The river spirit, Kubire-Oni, glided to the bank and knelt beside Sakura, reflecting the girl's slumped stance and bent head. At the same time, they looked to be twins and generations apart.

'Why are we here?' Sakura asked, drying her face for more tears to fall.

'I thought you might want to fix that pottery,' Kubire-Oni said, his rasping words catching on his sharp teeth on the way out of his mouth.

'What?'

Kubire-Oni delved his hands into the river and picked out the pieces of the pottery that had smashed when Sakura's father had slammed the door. How did they get here? Her mother had silently fixed it, returned it to the shelf, and carried on with a smile.

Kubire-Oni tore some white thread from the end of his tattered gown. It bent in the wind until it turned to gold. He handed her the pottery and the gold.

'Fix it whilst I tell you why we're here,' Kubire-Oni said, gliding his hand over the river to calm its ripples into a sheet of water.

Sakura began the art of kintsugi by filling in the gaps and cracks of the pottery with the gold and slotting the broken pieces together. When the gold could not hold such a large chip, she would thread the gold through the solidified clay until the two pieces would connect and not drift apart.

'This is the place I taught your mother to do that. She was here for quite a while. It was special for her to be here and feel like the river understood her,' Kubire-Oni said. 'The Kamo River holds lots of history. It is the birthplace of Kabuki.'

'Performance with face make-up,' Sakura answered. Their lavish face-paint had always unsettled her father, so Sakura and her mother would wash off their renditions hours before he was due to arrive home.

'A woman started it. Now it's performed only by men. But Akari would paint crimson lipstick in the shape of a smile across her cheeks and dance in the shallow waters here at night.'

Sakura placed the fixed pottery bowl beside her, the gold thread that held it together showing the evidence of breakage. Some saw it as beautiful. Sakura knew the difference between fixed and unbroken. Fixed is enough for something to function, like a computer or arcade game — not a person. She could not stop crying and her tears began to fill the mended bowl.

Sakura ran her fingernails across the half-clotted gashes in her wrist where the glass bottle had torn at her skin, the bottle she used to escape Shōjō, the bottle her father used to stay in the spirit's trance. She lifted her blood-coated fingers to her lips and drew a smile on her sagging face. In the water, she tried to get her lips to reach that line, but it was a twisted smile that didn't fit right on her face.

'You look like your mother,' Kubire-Oni said, reaching across to Sakura's face to pull the corners of her lips down for her so that she was frowning behind the red, perfectly shaped, false smile painted on her face like Kabuki make-up.

'My father never looks like this,' Sakura said, tracing her red smile in the water.

'Men are allowed to not smile,' sighed Kubire-Oni.

Sakura looked down at the pottery she had fixed as she said, 'Maybe he just doesn't know how to fix himself?'

'Do you know how to fix yourself?' the spirit asked.

'I thought I just did,' she said, picking at the crusted blood smile on her face.

Kubire-Oni laughed, his long scarlet tongue dangling from his parted lips.

Sakura looked at the clay bowl again. If the gold fixed it but showed scars of breakage, her painted smile showed how broken she was. She picked at her skin until the bloody patchwork flaked into the river.

'I'm allowed to not smile!' she cried.

Sakura's tears stopped falling, but somehow, she felt hollower this way — like she had nothing left to give. She washed her fingernails and wrists but could not find the energy to stand from the river's bank. The spirit lifted from his knees. A door had appeared on his stomach, a waterfall parted by his water-formed hands, his ivory gown torn down the middle, begging to be restitched with gold thread.

'Your mother was never able to accept that,' he said, twisting the polished brass handle that was attached to his body. He opened his arms wide for Sakura, and she stepped into his embrace.

***

She stepped through the door in Kubire-Oni's stomach and re-entered the world she knew, standing in one of the sink basins in the girls' toilets of the cemetery. The door behind her had already shut and locked itself, returning back to a mirror.

She hopped down onto the floor and, on tiptoes, peered through the frosted glass window into the cubicles. The faded image of Aka Manto draped in his red cloak smiled at her and waved from behind the closed door. She waved before turning her back on the kind spirit. But this was not a goodbye like her mother's. In time, she knew he would lead her through Grief once again.

She found her father slumped against her mother's gravestone with his forearm propped on his leg. From one hand hung a plastic bag, stamped with the logo of the local shop only a few minutes away. In the other, he held a fresh bottle of Goban Golden Ale.

'Good,' Hiroto said, taking a slow swig from the half-empty bottle, 'you've finally stopped crying.'

He handed Sakura her red school jacket, bought three sizes too big for her to grow into, which she draped over her shoulders. It wasn't too cold yet.

Sakura grabbed the beer bottle from her father's hand and

replaced it with her smaller one. As she led him down the path away from her mother's grave, she chucked the bottle into a bin. He would not drive Sakura away as he had his wife.

Pain sighed out through every pore of her body as she stretched her scarlet lips into a smile. A phantom wind clipped the edges of her red cloak.

Nos Da, Popstar

Joshua Jones

Chloe sits on the edge of the bed in a damp towel. She looks at the room she's tried to make her own, that still feels like a stranger's room.

With every husband her mother has married she's had a new bedroom, a new representation of herself each time. There used to be lots of pink, then walls covered in so many posters you couldn't see the paint underneath. Over the years there were posters of the Jonas Brothers, 5 Seconds of Summer, then McBusted. One Direction too, fresh-faced, baby fat and brimming with potential, only to be replaced by posters ripped out of *Kerrang!* magazine when she went through that weird goth phase. Now, there's a poster of Harry Styles, tattooed, broad-backed and gorgeous, next to an *American Psycho* poster. She has never seen it, but she thinks Christian Bale looks fit in a suit. And her favourite one: Elizabeth Fraser of Cocteau Twins, floppy-haired and ethereal, standing in front of her bandmates. Her dad got her into Cocteau Twins, and turned her on to other iconic musicians from the eighties and nineties, like Björk and Grace Jones. All posters in frames; she's an adult now. And Peter doesn't want his walls marked, anyway.

There are pictures tacked to the wardrobe door of Chloe, her sister Lottie, Bertie, and their mother on the beach at Barry Island. One of her, Bertie post-transition and Lottie, dressed up for Chloe's eighteenth birthday. There are pictures of Chloe and her friends at the old Elli cinema before it closed, and pictures in the new Odeon. Pictures from prom, the last day of school, college, pictures of Chloe's father, her sister's wedding and her mother's four. There's a space where a picture has been yanked off, remnants of Blu Tack, a pale square that hadn't seen sunlight before the room became hers, a year ago.

Her phone lights up with a notification from her astrology app: *The Sun enters Leo tonight*! She opens the app and reads her horoscope:

Now is the time to put yourself forward, Leo; spread your joy and generosity and you will receive joy and generosity in return.

From the 22nd of this month you may feel active, energetic — enjoy it! The New Moon on the 23rd and the Sun–Mars alignment on the 26th will only add to your power. This is the perfect time to make positive changes in your life.

She drops her phone back on the bed and towels her hair dry. Maybe, she thinks, now is the time for change. She feels ready for it. And she's practised for it every night — in the garage that holds Peter's tools and workbench, shelves of paint and thinner, the washing machine and dryer, a sink with its plughole coated in various forms of dried whatever. This dusty room separated from the house, smelling faintly of washing-up liquid and damp, this is where she can sing without anybody listening, and where she's practised her song for tonight's show. Chloe looks at her hair in the mirror and wishes she'd allowed her mother to put it in curlers earlier. I'd be prettier if my hair was curlier, she thinks. She wraps a lock of her hair around a finger and admires how dark it looks when it's wet and wishes this was her natural hair colour. She watches her hair limply fall onto her shoulders.

— How you feeling, love? Angie asks at the door.

The sun is beginning to set past the window, soon to be out of sight behind the apple trees, burdened with apples not yet ripe enough to be picked. The sky is peachy, not dissimilar to the watercolours Chloe paints just to discard, which Angie lovingly fetches out of her waste bin and keeps in a box under her bed.

— Yeah, alright. Chloe looks up from painting her middle toe, at her mother's kind, heavy face. Bit nervous.

— I get that, love. Angie sits on the edge of the bed. You'll be fine now. Just take a deep breath before you get up there and then just go for it and sing your heart out, yeah? She leans in and kisses Chloe's forehead. You'll be amazing. And remember, it's for charity. Just a bit of fun.

— I know, Mum, thanks. She hunches over her foot, carefully painting her little toe.

— I can't find the video camera. Don't suppose you've seen it anywhere?

— Why do you need it?

— Would like to have my own video of you, is all.

— There'll be someone there to video it, anyway. Think the last time I remember we used it was the wedding?

— Nah, pretty sure we got it out on our anniversary last month? But have no bloody idea where it could've gone.

— Well, to be fair, Mum, you and Pete were hammered.

— Oh, shush, you.

When she leaves, Chloe sighs and walks over to her dresser to inspect the makeup she owns. Her long hair, almost dry, hangs gracefully down to the small of her back. Over the years she has never been interested in makeup but has somehow acquired a tiny mountain of the stuff. Mostly from birthdays and Christmases, and yet, only recently she's begun to care for makeup. She applies a thin covering of moisturiser — Celestial by Lush, vanilla, almond oil and orchid extract — and fills out her eyebrows after carefully plucking a handful of rogue hairs. She's learned, more than anything, strong eyebrows go a long way. No one needs to contour their nose, or wear highlighter or anything like that, if they know how to work their eyebrows. Next is blush, a very small amount to accentuate her naturally rosy cheeks. She thinks about putting on lipstick. A coral-coloured satin stick from Nyx called Day Club, maybe, or a cherry-black colour? Instead she opts for balm to make her lips look dewy and soft.

She gets dressed quickly, in jeans and a white crop top with embroidered daisies on the chest. She wears small, simple hoop earrings and a chain her dad gave her last Christmas. She had sent her dad a text just before her shower, and her phone lights up as she knots the laces of her pastel yellow Vans, the trainers carefully picked to match the embroidered daisies and painted nails.

Ill be there, dont u worry. Running a bit late tho. Will be there before ur on. Cant wait. U wil smash it. Dad x.

***

The roads are busy as Peter drives through the town, and they seem to hit every red light. At the Halfway crossroads they inch forward. The stop light seems to last for minutes while the green only seconds. There's a child in the back of a black Toyota next to them who won't stop staring at Chloe and she smiles back. They drive through Parc Trostre and past

McDonald's where they see a long line of cars queueing for the drive-thru. Peter looks forlornly out the window, at the banner tied to the wooden fence advertising their new burger range, but they press on.

— Just got a text from Lottie, Chlo. She can't come tonight. Says one of the boys is ill. She's gutted.

— Aw, bless. Tell her not to worry.

— Auntie Janet will be there too. She's excited to see you sing, love.

— Yeah, it'll be nice.

Chloe looks out the window at the setting sky, peach and golden still, and the red glow of sidelights and brakes. Not a cloud in sight. It has been another hot summer's day without wind, and she can feel her deodorant clinging to her skin. She shaved her armpits in the shower, and a razor nick is beginning to sting, irritated by her nervous sweating. In a year or two, she could be in the back seat, like she is now, but it'll be a limo, or at least a very nice car, being driven to her show at St David's Hall, or somewhere else just as massive. Or even the O2 in Bristol, and all her newly devoted Welsh fans will flock there on trains just to hear her sing her songs. It'll be a long day of radio interviews, talking about her success, which started off playing a charity show in her hometown called *Nos Da, Popstar*, and how her team and record label are amazing, how they're helping her put the finishing touches on her debut album. And honestly, she can't thank them enough – for the opportunities, for the studio time, all the incredible musicians she's been able to work with. The cover of the album will be her, in black and white, looking defiantly into the camera, in homage to other massive popstars like Madonna and Adele. She won't be crammed into the back of a silver Ford Fiesta, the footwells covered in newspapers and fast-food wrappers.

They cross the roundabout for the turning and pull into the car park.

Chloe gets out and looks around as Peter helps Angie to her feet. A line of mopeds outside Dominos, drivers idling with their helmets under their arm, staring at their phones. There's still a light on at the Lexitan tanning salon, where her mother and the girls go for their tans. It's one of the few lights illuminating the car park. They make their way past the Travelodge — why would anyone want to stay in Llanelli? Chloe thinks, every time she walks past — and the Zion Baptist Church, once a beacon of community, until it was subsumed into the Ffwrnes Theatre. Now it stands, empty. She looks at the time on her phone and the screen reads 7.35 p.m. It's five minutes past doors.

The Ffwrnes Theatre, despite the greasy stink of cooked meats and chips in the air from the Hungry Horse opposite, is a glass cathedral of culture. There are a few people in evening dress already milling around behind the crystalline walls. Peter and Angie chat idly as they make their way towards the door, Chloe trailing behind, suddenly feeling very small, and a little bit silly in her jeans and T-shirt. She should have made more of an effort with her hair, put a bit more makeup on, worn a—

— Hiya, Chlo!

Sophie hugs her tight around the waist before Chloe has a chance to clock her. Sophie pulls back, and Chloe's dismayed to see she is wearing a long, flowy skirt and a light jumper. She always looks good without trying, the sort who doesn't try to turn heads and doesn't need to. Maybe I should have worn a dress, Chloe thinks.

— You look great, Chlo. Love tha top.

— Thanks, Soph. Had such a mare getting dressed. She looks at her nails; one of them is already chipped. Does this outfit look okay?

— Hiya, love, Chloe's mother says, at her side. You here on your own?

— Oh, no. Brought Gareth with me. He's over there look. Sophie turns and waves at her boyfriend, her latest one, who in turn waves back, sat at a table minding their drinks and Sophie's purse.

She sits with her back to the door, sipping a Coke, worried no one will come, worried plenty of people will come, glancing over her shoulder at the front door, eyeing up people walking past through the glass wall, constantly checking her phone for texts from her dad, wondering when he will arrive. She half listens to Gareth talk about his new job at Argos, how it's a proper laugh, everyone he works with is mental. Sophie looks only mildly interested, nodding or laughing dryly when appropriate. He's quite handsome, cute dimples when he smiles. But Christ, he's boring. Sophie don't half know how to pick them, boys who are nowhere near her level, nowhere near how interesting she is. But, no matter how many books she reads, or the latest band she's into, her photographic talent, she already wants to settle. Let's just hope it's not Gareth, who is now talking about *Baby Driver*, saying its Edgar Wright's best film since *Scott Pilgrim vs. the World*. What's worse, Chloe thinks — his wilful ignorance of Kevin Spacey's history of abuse, or his taste in film?

While Gareth is droning on about one of his co-workers, who is just *proper mental*, a stagehand appears from behind a door marked PRIVATE: STAFF ONLY. She has a radio strapped to her belt. She carries a clipboard and has a ponytail. She has authority.

— Evening, ladies and gentlemen. We'll be opening the doors very shortly. There'll be someone to help you to your seats. So, get the drinks in and we'll see you soon! Any performers who aren't backstage yet, please follow me.

Everyone listens to the young woman with the clipboard and rushes to the bar in a flurry of movement. Metal chair legs scraping against the floor. The muffled rustles of blazers and jackets picked up from the back of chairs and transferred to an arm. The sounds of men's shoes clapping the floor, probably the same shoes they wear for work or to church, poking out from the ends of shapeless blue jeans. Aunt Janet can be heard over the entire commotion, saying she needs a fag before the show starts, clip-clopping to the entrance. Chloe grabs the CD with her song on it from her mother and rushes over to the stagehand, her fingers numb, anxiety sweat breaking across her back.

— Hiya, I'm Chloe Matthews. I'm a singer.

— Ah yes, I have you here. She taps her clipboard. You ready? Feeling good?

Chloe quietly follows her through the staff door and into a backstage area where a boy in a plain white shirt, the sleeves rolled up to just below the elbow, is tuning an acoustic guitar. He has a tattoo on his forearm of the words *How soon is now?* on a gravestone. He looks up from his guitar and smiles at her. His teeth are white and shiny like in a toothpaste advert. Who smiles with teeth at a stranger? The stagehand is saying her name is Sarah and she'll be making sure everything runs smoothly backstage. She tells her the running order of the acts, but Chloe struggles to keep up over the sound of a comedian loudly practising his jokes, reading them from his phone. A drag queen peers out from behind the curtain at the crowd beginning to take their seats, tutting to herself, over people's (mostly men's) fashion choices. Among the blazers and shit jeans there are polo shirts with the collar popped, cargo shorts, flip flops — look at that skanky bloke wearing flip flops to the theatre, I'd rather die — and one or two in work clothes, covered in paint.

— Have you got your music with you, Chloe? Okay, great! the stagehand says, taking the CD from her.

A tall man in a dark red suit is ushered to the curtain, towering over the stagehands who offer him water and chewing gum, holding their hand up for him to wait while they look past the curtain to see if the crowd is fully seated. He looks like a caricature of showbiz. He smiles widely at each performer before strolling onto the stage. Chloe watches him through a crack in the curtain. It's a smaller room on the side of the actual theatre which can hold hundreds of people. There's a spotlight and a microphone stand in the centre of the beam, which the host grabs and rocks back and forth like he's Elvis.

— Good evening, ladies and gentlemen! Settle down, settle down now. Welcome to *Nos Da, Popstar*! Tonight, we have a burning display of talent to offer you, of music, laughs and more! I am your host for the night and as you know, my name is Stephen Jenkins. We have a full house tonight! And that means, we've managed to raise £1,500 for Cancer Research. Give yourself a round of applause!

The crowd claps, whoops and whistles. The host claps too, looking very pleased with himself. He smiles, and Chloe catches a glint of a gold tooth past the too-perfect lips. Is that lip filler? Christ, don't let Lottie get hold of him. She'll be dying to know his surgeon's number.

— Right, let's get to it then, shall we? Let me introduce to you our first guest, the fantastic and very funny Jon Barrison!

The man who'd been practising his lines from his phone wobbles over to the curtain and Chloe steps back to let him pass. He trips over the cloth and stumbles onto the stage. The crowd laughs and he raises his hand in a gesture of both greeting and self-acknowledgment. As he reaches the microphone, Chloe sees beads of sweat on his forehead in the spotlight glare.

— Can anyone tell me why Llanelli is like an orgy? he spits. The audience is silent. His shaking hand on the microphone stand causing it to vibrate.

— There's a lot of arseholes!

A few laughs, a couple of weak chuckles. Chloe sees Peter is one of the only ones who does a full belly laugh. She sees her brother Bertie come in late and dash over to where their mother has kept a seat for him. Jon stutters through another couple of jokes with varying degrees of success. He tells a story of going to AA just for a cup of tea, how Nando's plain chicken is too spicy for him. There are a few topical ones too, mostly about Brexit, but his delivery is off. He's choking on his words and spitting them out. As he waves goodbye someone in the audience shouts SEE YOU! and Stephen Jenkins meets him halfway across the stage to shake his hand.

— Put your hands together for Jon Barrison! Funny bloke, ain't he? He smiles a cheesy TV presenter smile. Now, don't forget that although tonight is for charity, it's still a contest. Yes, that's right, there's prizes to be won for first and second place. No prizes for third though, I'm afraid! Just a bit of fun, eh? He winks at no one in particular. With no further ado, I present to you our celebrity impersonator for the night!

He promptly carries the microphone to the side of the stage and exits past the curtain while the crowd is clapping, more out of obligation than genuine excitement. The impersonator drags her feet to centre stage, one hand on the small of the back, huffing with exertion, the other hand rearranging her massive breasts, possibly fake, fake as in costume dress, both hands in marigold gloves. She carries a cloth and cleaning liquid, tucked into a pocket on the front of her apron, and a headset microphone. She starts performing a routine of calling the audience *silly little bitches*, and says *piss off, darling* while squirting the cleaning liquid into thin air and pretending to wipe something down. She is Kim Woodburn having a *Big Brother*-esque breakdown while cleaning — clever to bring the two together like that — and the audience is loving it. Chloe sees her mother and Aunt Janet cracking up in their seats, Jan almost spilling her wine. Sophie is doubled over. And Gareth is laughing too, with his hand over his mouth, and frankly, Chloe is surprised; the guy really is fucking boring.

The audience erupt into applause as Kim Woodburn bows. Stephen walks out once again and theatrically stares at the audience in disbelief, as if dumbstruck by her talent. He makes a show of looking for the microphone stand and bringing it back to centre stage. Chloe grabs a bottle of water from a pack she assumes is for the performers and hears him tell the crowd to settle down, settle down.

— Alright then! Now, we have one last performer before we have a short break. And I want to say one more time: this is a competition! So, write down your winner and your second spot on the cards you've been given as the evening goes on. Let me present you with our next act, the beautiful Chloe Matthews!

— Good luck! The stagehand whispers.

She feels a gentle push on the small of her back and then her feet are walking her from behind the curtain onto the stage as if they belong to someone else. She doesn't resist, and takes the presenter's waiting hand automatically, gazes up at his dazzling smile, his careful quiff. He must have noticed her, a startled doe, because he leans in and whispers good luck in her ear. His breath is wet on her cheek.

Suddenly, she's alone. On a stage only a foot or so off the floor. And tiny, really; you could just about fit a full band on here. It may as well be infinite. Her tongue feels swollen. She gulps, looking out at the wall of black behind the spotlight. She can just make out her family at the front, her mum with phone poised. Is her dad here? The microphone is too tall for her, she struggles with the stand to bring it lower.

— Hiya, she says. She blinks in the sharp flash of a camera. She can smell her sweat, hot under the lights. She raises a trembling thumbs up in the direction of the curtain.

The opening bars of 'Heaven or Las Vegas' pump through the speakers, unmixed, unsure. The percussion bounces off the hard floors, but someone turns down the music slightly, just enough to take away the edge. The dreamy soundscape rolls gently under the looping drum machine, softer now, and Chloe counts herself in, then the opening verse. Shit, she sounds awful. That was shit, that whole verse. Alright, power through, not too much power, softly now. By the time she gets to the end of the first chorus she has her voice under control. She holds the mic stand with both hands, leaning in slightly. This must be what it's like to be in a movie, she thinks.

She feels the vibration in her sternum. The wall of black has closed in, encompassing the spotlight, and now it's just her in a fever dream of swirling skirts and long-exposure shots of disco lights and fog-machine mist. She sees fireworks in slow motion behind her eyelids and grips the mic with white knuckles. Her voice soars along the walls of guitar, soft and breathy at first, before hitting the audience with the full force of her wide, soprano range on the final chorus. They cheer and whistle but she doesn't notice them. She makes it to the end of the song, the music dies, and she sees, for the first time, the crowd are on their feet, sharing this moment with her. It feels like a TV moment, like *X Factor*, when an auditionee looks like they're going to be shit, but they smash it.

— Pretty brave of you to sing Cocteau Twins, the boy with the guitar says to her, after she's made her way backstage.

— Is it?

— Yeah, Liz Fraser got a hell of a voice on her. Pretty hard to sing her songs, seeing as no one really knows what she's saying.

— Yeah, I guess, she shrugs. I just sang the lyrics on Google.

— You did her justice, I reckon. I'm Tom, by the way. He offers her his hand to shake.

Bit formal. Must be nervous, bless him, she thinks.

— I'm Chloe, nice to meet you, she says, taking the hand. His palms are clammy and gross. She resists the urge to wipe her hand on her jeans after he's let it go. So, what songs are you playing? You singing as well?

— Yeah, mostly Smiths covers.

— Ah, explains the tattoo, she points to his forearm. I think that's braver than singing Liz Fraser. Bit racist, ain't he?

— Yeah. He rubs the tattoo with his hand. The Smiths still have tunes though. And them out there won't mind. He jabs a thumb in the direction of the curtain.

— Hmm, I guess.

— Got any tattoos yourself?

— Just the one. An opera mask on my leg.

— Nice. Sounds cool.

— Yeah, anyway, I got to go see my mum quick. Good luck with your set, yeah?

— Oh, I also wanted to ask, maybe you'd like to jam

sometime? He is blushing, conscious of how lame 'jam' sounds. Like, if you want to sing and I play guitar, or something?

— Yeah, sounds fun.

She exits to the bar and makes a beeline for her mum and Bertie, waiting for her by the window. On the other side of the glass is a small line of smokers, Aunt Janet waving her arms flamboyantly, telling some tall tale or other. She catches Chloe's eye and waves, turns to a woman next to her and mouths something. There are the familiar sounds of hard soles squeaking on the floor and glasses clinking, conversation fading into ambient noise. Someone stops her on the way to where her family are standing and congratulates her on singing. She takes the compliment, thinking it's weird to say well done to someone for singing. The smell of chicken, peri-peri and chip fryers breezes through every time the front doors are thrown open.

— Fucking hell, that was amazing, Chlo! Bertie pulls her in for a tight hug. He's wearing strong aftershave, Paco Rabanne or something. It catches at the back of her throat. Felt like the song was your own.

— Yeah, well done, love, her mother says. You were stunning. Had a tear in my eye and everything. She reaches up to give Chloe a sloppy kiss on the cheek. She seems subdued, quiet.

— Thank you, yeah, I'm pleased. She rubs at the moist mark of her mother's kiss. Fucked it a little at the beginning, but I think it went well, she says. Everything alright, Mum? You seem a bit quiet.

— I'm, I'm... Her jaw wobbles and she blinks like she's about to cry. I'm being bloody emotional, sorry love. That was just really lovely.

Angie wipes at her eyes. Bertie rubs her arm and rolls his eyes at Chloe.

— Do you know if Dad is here, Mum?

— I haven't seen him, love. Was he meant to be here?

— I text him. He said he was coming.

— That fucking man, honestly, I —

— Don't start, Mum, says Bertie.

Chloe can hardly focus for the rest of the show. Tom wails through 'This Charming Man' and 'Bigmouth Strikes Again', attempting to imitate Morrissey's baritone croon. The result sounds like he's chewing through a mouthful of cotton wool. He gets the crowd to sing along though, finishing with 'How Soon Is Now?' The crowd clap and cheer him off politely.

Stephen Jenkins returns to the stage once again and announces the prizes: a headline gig and £100 for the winner, a family voucher for the Hungry Horse opposite for the runner-up. Then the drag queen takes to the stage, announced as Stacey Sinnamon, and she is powerful. She's a fury of stiletto heels, of towering legs and orange tinsel like golden gossamer silk. She dances and dazzles and makes the whole room gasp in unison as she drops into a perfect split. She sings and shines like a shooting star. The audience transfixed, drinks by their feet forgotten, hands raw from clapping. Mr Owen, from the *Llanelli Star*, lighting the queen with frantic camera flashes. She leaves the stage in a whirl of bows and curtsies, showering the audience with hand-blown kisses. The winner is decided. Just look at the room.

The host takes to the stage one last time and thanks the audience and the performers while the stagehands collect all the paper votes. He bangs on about all the great work Cancer Research Wales do and the theatre's upcoming events as the votes are counted. The winner is Stacey Sinnamon, followed by Chloe Matthews in second place. And suddenly she's on stage, bowing and thanking the audience, accepting vouchers for the Hungry Horse, and she and Stacey are embracing.

Backstage the stagehand from earlier says she was great, and they'll try to get her in for a gig, and Chloe says that would be great, thank you so much. One last handshake with Stephen. She and Stacey talk about *Ru Paul's Drag Race*, and how they hope it will come to the UK soon. Chloe says Stacey would be fierce on it. Stacey agrees. Then she accepts Tom's number, says she'll text him *for a jam*. There's more mingling in the bar, drinks, her mother still fuming at her dad's absence, but Chloe doesn't have the energy for it. Bertie whispers to Chloe that Stacey Sinnamon is the most amazing thing he's ever seen, and she says, Go talk to her, Bert, and he says he can't. But she urges him to, says he can have her Hungry Horse vouchers if he asks Stacey out. And he does, mopping his brow. They exchange numbers by the time everyone empties out of the theatre. Sophie brags to Gareth how she is certain Chloe's going to make it big. If anyone could get out of this shithole of a town, it would be Chloe Matthews. He nods like he isn't listening, or maybe he is. They get burgers on the way home, the sky shot through with stars and airplane lights. In the McDonalds drive-thru she receives texts from her father.

Author Biographies

Ruairi Bolton is a student at Swansea University, presently just having come out of his second year of an English Literature and Creative Writing degree. He lives in Essex, England, with parentage from Northern Ireland and an education in Wales. All he needs now is a pet from Scotland and he'll have the full set.

Ruby Burgin was born in 2001 and lives in Bristol with her family but made Swansea her home whilst studying English Literature and Creative Writing at university. Ruby enjoys playing piano and singing but her passion is writing, mainly fantasy and literary fiction. Now, post-graduation, she hopes to pursue her writing career. This is her first publication.

Bethan L. Charles migrated to Monmouthshire in 2022, close to her Cardiff roots. She is a Lecturer in Renewable Energy, but in her spare time she writes historical and speculative fiction. Her stories often focus on underrepresented voices in science and mythology. In 2022, she won Globe Soup's international short story competition and a Page Turner Writing Mentorship Award. Her words appear in *Globe Soup*, *The Copperfield Review*, and others. Find her @BLCharlesWrites.

JL George (she/they) was born in Cardiff and raised in Torfaen. Her first novel *The Word* won the New Welsh Writing Awards and Rubery Book Award and is published by New

Welsh Rarebyte. Her short fiction can be found in *New Welsh Reader, Gwyllion*, and various other magazines and anthologies. She currently works behind the scenes at Cardiff University library service, but in a previous life as an academic, wrote a PhD on classic weird fiction. You can find her on Twitter at @jlgeorgewrites and on Mastodon at @jlgeorge@toot.wales.

Joshua Jones (he/him) is a queer, autistic writer and artist from Llanelli, south Wales. He co-founded Dyddiau Du, a NeuroQueer art and literature space in Cardiff. His fiction and poetry have been published by Poetry Wales, Broken Sleep Books, *Nawr* Magazine and others. He is a Literature Wales Emerging Writer, 2023, and is currently working with the British Council to connect Welsh and Vietnamese queer writers. His publications include *Fistful of Flowers* (2022) and *Local Fires*, coming November 2023 from Parthian Books.

Emma Moyle grew up in the Swansea Valley. After completing an MA at the University of East Anglia, she moved to the Midlands, where she has been teaching English for 25 years. 'The Pier' is her first short story.

Rachel Powell was born in Caerphilly and grew up in the nearby village of Maesycwmmer. Harbouring a lifelong love of reading and writing stories, she studied Literature and Creative Writing with the Open University as a mature student, graduating with first-class honours in 2019. Since then, Rachel has had several short stories reach the shortlist stage in various competitions, and recently had a poem published for the first time in *Writers Forum* magazine. Rachel currently works as a supply library assistant while in the process of writing her first novel.

Matthew G. Rees grew up in the border country known as the Marches in a Welsh family with roots in both industrial and rural Wales. He has – among other things – been a journalist, a teacher, and a night-shift cab driver. His books include *Keyhole*, a collection of short stories set in Wales and the Marches (Three Impostors press, 2019). His most recent book is *The Snow Leopard of Moscow & Other Stories*, a collection set in Putin-era Moscow where Matthew lived and worked for a period. BAFTA-winning writer Stephen Volk has called him 'a master of concise not-a-word-wasted yet cinematic storytelling'.

Silvia Rose is a writer and tutor born and raised in Eryri. Having graduated with an English Literature and Creative Writing BA from the University of East Anglia, she now runs writing workshops in her local area and works as a freelancer. In 2021, she published her first poetry collection, *Spell into Being*, and is currently working on nonfiction projects. Her work has been published in *Planet* Magazine, *The Primer* and Musing Publications. In March 2023 she was named as one of Literature Wales's Emerging Welsh Writers. Her writing is largely inspired by her Welsh and Serbian roots.

Satterday Shaw has led writing workshops for adults (including women with long-term mental health problems) and teenagers (including Roma teenagers). She has worked in anti-racist education.

She writes fiction for adults and young adults. Her stories and articles have been published in *Meniscus, Mslexia, The London Magazine,* a Chawton House anthology, *Wasafiri, Michigan Feminist Studies, The Yellow Room, GM Fiction, Cree: Rhys Davies Short Story Anthology 2022, Wales Arts Review* and other publications. She lives in Eryri.

Emily Vanderploeg writes fiction and poetry. She studied Creative Writing at Swansea University (MA, PhD), and English and Art History at Queen's University (BA Hons), where she works as an online lecturer. Emily is a Hay Festival Writer at Work and recently completed a novel with the help of a Literature Wales New Writer's Bursary Award. Her poetry pamphlet, *Loose Jewels,* won the Cinnamon Press Pamphlet Competition and was published in 2020. *Strange Animals*, her debut collection of poetry, was published by Parthian Books in 2022. Originally from Aurora, Ontario, Canada, she lives in Swansea.

Dan Williams was born in The Midlands but spent his formative years just outside of Dolgellau, in the shadow of Cadair Idris. He draws inspiration for his stories from the juxtaposition of the external wilderness with the internal conflict of ordinary individuals. He is married with two daughters and enjoys exploring the hills and mountains with his Labrador, Elle. He currently lives in Worcestershire and teaches High School English, which doesn't allow much time for writing but does at least mean that he is surrounded by stories. He believes that teaching, if it's done right, is storytelling.

PARTHIAN

⊞ MODERN
Ⅲ WALES

RAYMOND WILLIAMS: A WARRIOR'S TALE

Dai Smith

Raymond Williams (1921-1998) was the most influential socialist writer and thinker in post-war Britain. Now, for the first time, making use of Williams' private and unpublished papers and by placing him in a wide social and cultural landscape, Dai Smith, in this highly original and much praised biography, uncovers how Williams' life to 1961 is an explanation of his immense intellectual achievement.

"Becomes at once the authoritative account... Smith has done all that we can ask the historian as biographer to do."
– Stefan Collini, *London Review of Books*

PB / £16.99
978-1-913640-08-8

FURY OF PAST TIME: A LIFE OF GWYN THOMAS

Daryl Leeworthy

This landmark biography tells the remarkable story of one of modern Wales's greatest literary voices

HB / £20
978-1-914595-19-6

PARTHIAN

RHYS DAVIES

RHYS DAVIES: SELECTED STORIES

Rhys Davies

"Gently wrapped, these stylish perceptive tales have centres as hard as steel, and are all the better for it."
– *William Trevor,* The Guardian

£8.99 / PB
978-1-912109-78-4

RHYS DAVIES: A WRITER'S LIFE

Meic Stephens

"This is a delightful book, which is itself a social history in its own right, and funny."
– The Spectator

£11.99 / PB
978-1-912109-96-8

PARTHIAN

Fiction

Take a Bite:
The Rhys Davies Short Story Award Anthology

ISBN 978-1-913640-63-7
£9.99 • Paperback

**THE TWELVE WINNERS OF THE
2021 RHYS DAVIES SHORT
STORY AWARD**

Cree:
The Rhys Davies Short Story Award Anthology

ISBN 978-1-914595-23-3
£10 • Paperback

**THE TWELVE WINNERS OF THE
2022 RHYS DAVIES SHORT
STORY AWARD**

PARTHIAN   Short Stories

Figurehead
CARLY HOLMES
ISBN 978-1-912681-77-8
£10.00 • Paperback

'Through beautiful, rhythmic prose
Figurehead weaves a sequence of stories
that are strange, captivating, and
unforgettable.' – Wales Arts Review

Love and Other Possibilities
LEWIS DAVIES
ISBN 978-1-906998-08-0
£6.99 • Paperback
'Davies's prose is simple and effortless, the
kind of writing that wins competitions.'
– *The Independent*

Local Fires
JOSHUA JONES
ISBN 978-1-913640-59-0
£10.00 • Paperback

'In this stunning series of interconnected
tales, fires both literal and metaphorical
blaze together to herald the emergence of a
singular new Welsh literary voice.'

Whatever Happened to Rick Astley?
BRYONY RHEAM
ISBN 978-1-914595-14-1
£10.00 • Paperback

'skilled, perfectly formed, and compelling ...
a deeply satisfying collection'
– Karen Jennings

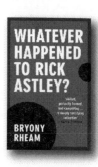